I MET MURDER

I MET MURDER

By

SELWYN JEPSON

THE MODERN PUBLISHING CO.

LONDON

MADE AND PRINTED IN GREAT BRITAIN BY PURNELL AND SONS, LTD.
PAULTON (SOMERSET) AND LONDON

THIS manuscript was found on Mr. John Arden's desk in the library at Eastblyth Manor within a few minutes of his being shot dead. Mr. George Jupp, later Detective Inspector, C.I.D., who was investigating the Eastblyth murders, took possession of the manuscript. His permission to publish it has recently been obtained.

S. J.

CHAPTER I

THE WINE-GLASS in my hand dropped its stem on to the plate in front of me with a small crash which startled everybody at the table. At precisely the same moment something hit the panelling behind my head, causing a faint but definite thud. I jumped a little, and cried out. Who could have helped it?

Conversation stopped abruptly, and the five people who were dining with me stared with expressions of surprise and question. Jeames came forward from the sideboard to relieve me of what was left of the wine-glass. He was obviously pained, for, as a good butler, he expected every wine-glass of his to do its duty, not to fall to pieces in a man's hand.

"Close the windows, and the curtains!" I said, and probably because there was a certain urgency in my tone, he forgot his usual deliberacy of movement, and almost hurried to the french windows.

When the peaceful, moonlit garden, with its wide lawn and dark background of trees, disappeared behind the curtains, I relaxed. These things had occupied only a few seconds in their happening, but they were seconds of tension. A breaking wine-glass and a mysterious thud against a wall are not normal occurrences at a dinner-party.

Professor Skinner stirred the momentary silence. His thin, clever face was grim, and his long mouth twisted up in one corner, interrogatively.

"Bullet?" he said. "Someone trying to end your interesting life, Arden? Damned if it wasn't pretty close to you—that wine-glass——"

The effect of the word "bullet" on my other guests was immediate and to be expected. Lady Codrington, red-haired and neurasthenic, repeated it in a shrill squeak; Hamish Page, the financier, dropped his fish fork with a clatter, and everybody

7

looked from me to the window, and back again. Their expressions were various, but all alarmed.

"It's all right!" I said quickly. "Perhaps it was only a stone."

"Stone, my eye!" muttered Hamish Page nervously, and rose to his feet the better to pass his fat forefinger round the inside of his evening-dress collar. "Get police! Get police! Search the grounds! Won't do at all, that sort of thing! Won't do, I tell you——"

The Reverend Lionel Lake, on Lady Codrington's right, patted her hand.

"Yes, indeed. A stone, no doubt. Some mischievous boy—the young rascal! If it had been a—ah—bullet, shouldn't we have heard the—ah—sound of the shot? I must confess I heard nothing which——"

"Small-calibre rifle fitted with a silencer," suggested Professor Skinner, and, as an expert on armament, they listened to him with attention.

"I'm afraid I thought of that, too," I said, and I began searching the black oak panelling for signs of the bullet.

Anita Skinner, who had been the least upset of anyone, cried:

"What fun! 'Late extra-a! Attempted murder of John Arden, the eminent sociologist!' Things are brightening up in Eastblyth. I shan't bother to go to Dinard, now. Anyway it'll be as dull as ditch-water before the middle of June. I shall stay, and make love to the best-looking detective! Please, John, get me a young, handsome one."

The Reverend Lionel pursed his lips. The only thing in the world about which I agreed with him was Skinner's daughter. Her passionate demand for sensation—and it didn't matter what kind as long as there was plenty of it—was no less avid than her father's search for a quicker-firing and longer-ranged field gun. She was, as the Vicar put it, "a little hard, my dear Arden, a little hard." The description was kind. She was as tough as a tenpenny nail, and as sharp. Her remarks at that moment did not go down well. Apart from anything else, it

8

reminded us that Lady Codrington had eloped with a French marquis three summers ago, choosing Dinard for her setting.

"Oughtn't the servants to search the garden or something?" said Lady Codrington quickly, and smiled sweetly at Anita.

"Jeames will telephone the Sergeant at Eastblyth," I said reassuringly. "Here's the bullet. A bit flattened—this panelling has been here three hundred years, and it is by way of being hard. They used home-grown oak in those days."

I handed the fragment of lead to the Professor. The others stared at it with various and characteristic emotions: horror, excitement, fascination. Skinner, holding it between finger and thumb, screwed up his eyes at it, sideways, like a bird, and nodded his thin, bald head.

"That's no stone, Vicar." He dropped it on the table in front of the Reverend Lionel, who looked at it with round blue eyes. In the momentary silence I heard Jeames telephoning in the hall. Then the Professor added briskly:

"The base is still in its original shape—diameter unaltered, therefore. Undoubtedly a ·22. It certainly would seem as though you had an enemy, Arden."

"The wickedness of men!" cried the Vicar.

"All nice people have enemies," said Anita, and I wondered a little at the strained expression in her eyes. I caught but a glimpse of it. Was she more troubled about my narrow escape than she pretended? Must she never show her real feelings behind the mask of a bright young person?

"During the war," I said, "I did a certain amount of hush-hush work for the British Government, particularly in the final months. It is possible that there are one or two people who would quite cheerfully put me out if the opportunity was handy. It's mysterious. Was it an attempt to kill, or an effort to frighten?"

"I tell you, you ought to order a search of the garden at once!" growled Hamish Page, who had been recovering his composure with the aid of three quick glasses of Chablis. "An' if you'd have run out there immediately you might have seen the fellow!"

9

"The plan occurred to me," I said. "And it also struck me that if someone was trying to pick me off from the concealment of the trees, I couldn't give him a better chance of a second shot. The only sensible thing to do was to close the window and draw the curtains—which we did. The disadvantage in that, of course, lay in the fact that it told whoever was out there that we realised what had happened, and he, or she, bolted at once. To have tried to follow, even with weapons, would have been remarkably risky; and in any case it would have taken minutes to reach the gun-room, arm ourselves, and get out into the garden and the woods."

"Huh!" said Hamish Page, who because he had three and a half millions deemed manners unnecessary.

"Arden is perfectly right," commented the Professor. "Those were the only conclusions one could come to under the circumstances. One of the great advantages of a trained mind, taking a——"

But his daughter interrupted him, a thing she seldom ventured to do. In spite of her careless attitude toward life, she had a wholesale respect for her only surviving parent. Now, however, she leant forward, ignoring the fact that he was speaking.

"John, when you said just now, 'He, or she,' you had the idea it *might* be a woman?"

Again the anticipation, the appetite for a sensation. Her green eyes were feline; pouncing.

"In no particular sense," I said.

"A woman beat several records at Bisley this year," stated her father drily. "And Arden is always saying unkind, if true things about the sex in his lectures and pamphlets. As a sociologist, his work brings him constantly in touch with the weaknesses of our females. Think of the dozens who must loathe the very sound of his name! How many of them would not seize the chance to shoot him down? And feel privileged! They would not let themselves be softened by his good looks, his taste in wine, his ambition to make the world a better place to live in, or even by the innocence of his pleasures. His model carpenter's shop, his beautiful miniature lathe, and the devoted hours he spends with them would avail him nothing! Hell hath no fury like a woman about whom you have told the awful, economic truth!"

Hamish Page grunted, and said:

"For all you seem to care, Arden might be lyin' dead in that ancestral chair of his. This business isn't one to joke about. He might be dead, *dead*!"

"But he is not," the scientist pointed out; "and, further, he is behaving rationally. He refuses to lose his wits——"

He eyed Hamish Page unsympathetically. In Hamish the incident had produced a bad attack of nerves. Indeed I think it probable that but for the Professor's coolness, my weekly dinner-party to these my neighbours would have broken up there and then. As things were, however, the panic went out of them. Jeames returned from the telephone with the information that Sergeant Grice would leave the police-station for the scene of the shooting the moment he had warned his colleagues at Darsham and Southwold to keep a look-out for suspicious characters. Jeames delivered this message with a commendable lack of emotion, and thus poured further oil on the waters which had been so violently disturbed by that small but ominous piece of lead.

"Serve the bird," I said.

Hamish Page scowled to himself for a while, but presently subsided into a gloomy silence. I had often wondered how the man had managed to find the strength of mind and will to garner his vast fortune. Since he had bought Blyth Towers, and there set up an astonishing menage which even the most superior of the Suffolk county people admitted was worthy of the place, I had seen quite a lot of him, but I had never discovered the secret of his money-making *flair*. It was true he had made the larger part of his millions during the war, and to make them had ridden rough-shod over nearly every human decency. But even with the high war-time value of commodities and raw materials, and the possible advantages of under-paying those who worked for him, it must have required personal courage and a certain steadfastness of purpose to acquire such a fortune. Yet, as far as I could determine, he possessed nothing of those qualities. As a sociologist, and as somewhat of an idealist, it shocked me to think that mere ruthlessness and a modicum of cunning could raise a man so high, if only in things material, above his fellow men.

I am purposely taking Hamish Page at this point and examining him rather minutely, for reasons which later I hope to make clear. The others who dined with me on that important night must be analysed afterwards in their turn, if this exposition of the Eastblyth murders is to have any value— Professor Skinner, his daughter Anita, Lady Codrington, and the Reverend Lionel Lake pass for a moment from these pages save as names, but in a little time they will return as personalities whom I have had admirable opportunities of learning, and, I think, of learning accurately. George Jupp, himself an astute and experienced observer of human nature—and no great criminologist can be less—told me yesterday that my conclusions regarding these five people had helped him very materially in his investigation. I might mention here that it was that very remark of his, and the sincerity with which he made it, which decided me to write this account of the murders.

Forgive the digression—let us get back to our Hamish Page.

He ate his partridge greedily, and if one had not seen him eat his *sole meunière* with the same avidity, one might have suspected him of striving to settle the qualms of his stomach with sheer weight of food. No; he was of a naturally greedy temperament. He lived the way he ate. He was large of girth, short of stature, with thin, shining black hair which was drawn meticulously from one side of his head across to the other to hide a shameful baldness on the top. It failed in this, and bright-pink Hamish Page gleamed through the oiled lines of hair. His nose was long and straight to find in so round a face, but his small, oval mouth was more in keeping with the type. He must have been a trial to his tailor and his valet, for he had no natural aptitude for wearing the kind of clothes they insisted upon. He would have preferred to go his way collarless; I had never seen him really at ease with one.

The best description I can apply to him which may briefly show him is that of a perfect type of war profiteer, more perfect even than the popular and fictional notion of one. If he had had a wife, she would have been as fat as himself, and her diamonds would have yapped and glittered offensively to high Heaven. But he was unmarried, although at this time in danger of matrimony, an aspect of the business I shall deal with in due course. He dwelt alone at Blyth Towers, three miles from this house, and the number of his servants, secretaries and assistant secretaries was legion. These were mostly women, and amongst the secretaries there were some astonishingly good-looking ones. People, in particular those who found his vulgarity unpalatable but not so his food —for they ate it in quantity at the many dinners and parties he gave—suggested that Hamish couldn't possibly require so many secretaries, and asked meaningly why did you never see an ugly one?

There may have been an element of justice in the insinuation, but that was a matter for the secretaries. It was unsavoury, if you like, but typical, of course, of the man.

About the countryside, he was cordially disliked, because he was mean in those small ways in which a millionaire is expected by the ignorant to be generous; whilst amongst the gentry he was despised rather than disliked. They accepted and returned his hospitality, however, and one met him at dinner-parties, where he was tolerated amiably enough. There was no nonsense about him, they said; he realised he lacked polish, education and the social graces, and, to his credit, made no effort to affect these things. If he felt like being rude, he was rude. He possessed about three and a half million pounds.

For the last eight months, since the time he had come to Eastblyth from Nottinghamshire, or wherever it was he had collected the millions, he had dined regularly with me once or twice a month, and I had gone over to Blyth Towers, to dinners or garden-parties about the same number of times. I liked having him to the manor because he took a pleasure in February. And I believe I would have, if it had come to the he went out, and because he annoyed people like Lady Codrington, who was a snob, if an ill-behaved one.

He rarely, if ever, opened his mouth except to put edible or drinkable substances into it, but to-night, when he had dealt faithfully with the partridge, he gulped down a quarter of a pint of Château Lafitte 1911, and spoke. He dropped a large rock into the quietening waters, and set them splashing again. He said:

"They shot at *me* last night."

Again there was that tense, expectant, startled silence. The Vicar, who had just delivered a particularly unctuous truism, which I have forgotten, cried:

"Shot at you! Dear me!"

"Where did this happen?" asked Skinner.

"More and more fun!" added Anita. "Anybody else been potted?"

Hamish Page glanced at her reproachfully.

"They got a damn sight too near me to be comfortable, I tell you. Right over my head as I was having coffee after dinner on the terrace. It wasn't a hornet, or one of them kind of insects. It was a blasted bullet out of a gun!" He glowered at the Professor, as being in principle responsible for all forms of artillery.

"Rifle," Skinner remarked. "Rifle. Did you save the bullet?"

"It banged into a window just behind me, and smashed a hole through it," said the financier, "that's how I knew it wasn't one of them hornets. I couldn't find the bullet, though. I didn't want to. I locked the door and got into bed. Felt better about it in the morning—decided it was a poacher tryin' to pick off a roostin' pheasant. But after this—to-night I'm thinkin' it was a different kind of poacher, pickin' off a different kind of bird. I don't know how Arden stands for enemies, but I've got a few, I can tell you. An' if you ask me, it's the same fella tryin' to scare us both."

It had been fairly obvious for the last six weeks that Hamish Page wanted more than casual friendship from Skinner's daughter; he was fifty-eight, and had decided, a trifle late, that the time had come for him to find a wife. He was pretty well in love with her, in a heavy, rather maudlin and middle-aged way, but as yet Anita had shown no desire for a sensation like Hamish Page. It was considered, however, that in time she would. Three and a half millions were three and a half millions. They would buy her a good deal of excitement, one way and another. In the meantime she was doing what the Americans call "stringing him along." He did not seem to mind; he was used to getting what he wanted; he'd get Anita. You could see that.

"All this," I said after a pause in which we digested matters, "is rather odd. I don't know what you feel, Skinner?"

He also was puzzled.

"Why should the same person want to frighten or kill, whichever the idea is—two men like yourselves who until recently, I believe, had never met; whose lives, occupations, interests and activities have been along widely separated ways?"

"Echo answers why," said Anita with a remarkable return of her former cheerfulness.

"The man who is going to tell me why," stated Hamish Page rather aggressively, "will know more than I do. An' the sooner the police get movin', the happier I'm goin' to be. Where's that sergeant? I tell you there's *murder* about!"

Lady Codrington squeaked slightly, and gazed fearfully at the financier. The others looked again at the window, where the drawn curtains and closed doors seemed less reassuring than they had been.

"I'm not a nervous man," remarked our Hamish, but without any great air of conviction. His small eyes were restless.

The Reverend Lionel coughed.

"We must have strength—we must not let the powers of evil have sway over us."

"A ·22 rifle fitted into a silencer has certainly a power of evil when it's in the wrong hands," observed the Professor, who was a practical man.

The Vicar sighed, and without warning began to recite in slow, measured tones that thing in "The Masque of Anarchy":

> *"I met Murder on the way—*
> *He had a mask like Castlereagh,*
> *Very smooth he looked, yet grim.*
> *Seven bloodhounds followed him."*

"Dammit!" said the financier irritably, "you're a helpful fella, eh? Helpful——"

The Reverend Lionel was at once overcome with contrition. Hamish Page was going to rebuild the chancel.

"My dear sir!" cried the Vicar. "I assure you I——"

"All right, all right, all right!"

Then Sergeant Grice arrived on a bicycle, and we conducted a perfunctory and fruitless search of the wood. Obviously my would-be assassin had decamped. In the daylight on the morrow we would look for traces of him.

Whether the chancel of Eastblyth Church is ever rebuilt or not, one thing is certain; Mr. Hamish Page will not sign the cheque which pays for it.

That same night, sometime between a quarter past twelve and seven o'clock next morning, the financier went to the window of his bedroom on the first floor of Blyth Towers, and while he stood there yet another bullet came singing through the peaceful moonlight.

His household, his servants, and his secretaries slept undisturbed by any sound from that silenced rifle, and no one went to his room until the morning, when at eight minutes past seven his valet took in the early tea.

The bullet, penetrating the millionaire's forehead, had pursued a straight course through the brain, and lodged in the parietal bone.

He must have been dead before he touched the floor.

CHAPTER II

"I THINK," said George Jupp with a kind of sigh, "that I ought to explain how I happen to appear in this affair, Mr. Arden. You say you know my name?"

I looked from the card to George Jupp, and told him that I had heard Bowers, of the Home Office, speak of George Jupp, the criminologist, and that since he wished to see me with regard to the death of Mr. Page, I deduced that he was Bower's "George." If there was anything I could do to help him in this dreadful affair, I would be only too pleased to place myself at his disposal.

"Very kind of you, Mr. Arden," he said gloomily. "It's a stupid kind of case, from my point of view, and I don't see how anybody can help anybody in it. Most unsatisfactory. Well, I came up to Eastblyth to-day because yesterday morning I received a letter from Mr. Page in which he said that his life was in danger from some unknown assailant, and would I be good enough to come to Blyth Towers and keep the danger at bay, as it were. Cheque for five hundred pounds, as a retainer. We all have to live, Mr. Arden, and in any case millionaires fascinate me. As I was packing my bag, the noon edition of the evening paper came in at the letter box, and the headlines told me that the danger had reached him before I had. That he was dead when I read his letter. Now I'm tolerably honest, and it seemed to me I ought to do something to earn that five hundred pounds. So I'm going to sit around and watch the police clear the thing up, at the same time seeing if I can't get a line on the why and wherefore . . ." He ambled on a little in a desultory monologue about the difficulty the police seemed to be in.

He was a small man, about fifty, of that pre-eminently English type which always looks thin and miserable when there is an east wind blowing. His colouring as to hair and eyes was indeterminate, a kind of mouse-blondeness, and his thin eyebrows pointed upward in the middle with a permanent, mildly aggrieved air. He wore a neat blue suit, pale blue shirt and collar, grey-blue tie, and beautifully kept and polished brown shoes. He struck me at once as a person of considerable education and breeding; I had never heard of any distinguished family of his name, but I felt that I would not be surprised to hear that there was one, and that George Jupp belonged to it. "Oh yes, a Lincolnshire Jupp, of course," or something like that. I wondered often, during the next ten days or so, what had turned him into a detective, a crime investigator; a curiosity, perhaps, which was largely due to the atmosphere of gloomy dissatisfaction in which the man moved and dwelt. He did not seem happy about himself.

"A stupid case," he repeated, and sighed again.

I gave him a cigarette, which he lit with meticulous care, as you and I would light a cigar, and went on:

"You see, Mr. Arden, a man like Hamish Page has done a great deal of damage to other people in the course of his life."

"He has certainly trodden on them," I agreed.

Jupp nodded.

"And taken their money when they were down. He must have made a quantity of enemies, of whom several might be capable of murdering him. The motive of revenge. That will be the police theory, I imagine. They have not proceeded far, of course—there has scarcely been time. Inspector English has —er—interviewed you?"

"At nine o'clock yesterday morning—before he saw anybody else," I replied. "You would like me to tell you everything I told him?"

"Just a moment. Have you any idea why the Inspector should have picked on you first?"

"Three good reasons, I should say. The first, that I am the sort of local Squire; the second, that Page dined here the night he was killed—the night before last, that is; and the third, that I had had cause to call in the police on account of an attempted murder earlier that same evening."

Jupp's gloom deepened.

"Attempt to murder whom?"

"Myself."

18

He sat up in his chair, and fixed his eyes on me.

"You were in business with Page, ever? Associated financially——?"

"Never in my life. I've only known him since he came to live in my neighbourhood, and by then he had retired. I have never been in business. I have a comfortable private income, and a profession."

"Sociologist," remarked Jupp. "Interesting subject. Student of humanity myself. I must say at first sight I couldn't see any connection between you and a man like Page which would make your joint murders reasonable to the same perpetrator —assuming, of course, that the two incidents, or rather three, counting the attempt the previous night on Mr. Page, appear to be related. I have learnt that he was shot at? Is that so?"

"Page told us at dinner that he had been shot at by a rifle fitted with a silencer—at least, that is what we deduced, since he heard no report. The bullet smashed a window after it had passed over his head. He told us this a few minutes after a bullet had been fired at me, during the fish. I was sitting at the head of the table. It was fired from the garden, probably from the shelter of that wood which you can see from here——"

"No sound of the shot?"

"Not a sound."

"Window was open?"

"Wide."

"Did the bullet come close?"

"It smashed a wine-glass in my hand, and partially flattened itself against the panelling about five inches to the right of my throat."

"Hum," said Jupp. "Show me."

I took him into the dining-room. I was able to demonstrate the exact position in which I had been sitting, for the carved, high-backed Charles II chair in which I sit at meals is too heavy to be casually moved. I showed Jupp the whitish mark on the black oak panelling where the bullet had struck.

"Close," he said sepulchrally. "Damned close. Looks more like a miss than a warning or effort to scare. Got the bullet?"

"The Inspector has it. I gave it to Sergeant Grice when he came up that night to deal with the matter."

"How did he deal with it?"

"He looked through the wood with his torch, and found nothing to show which way the fellow had gone, or where he had stood for that matter. The wood is walked over a good deal, you see, and there are a lot of little paths, and so on. He decided to return in daylight to search more thoroughly, but——"

"——didn't because of the killing at Blyth Towers. Natural enough. Now tell me, Mr. Arden. Who wants to slaughter you?"

"The Inspector asked me that," I replied, "and I have given the thing a lot of thought, both recently and at the time of the attempt. Ten years ago, at the end of the War, I could have named at least one man, and probably two, who would have been glad to remove me, if only for the satisfaction of knowing that I ceased to exist. But, as you know, the desire to avenge a wrong, however deep the wrong, does not often persist for ten years in anybody. In the case of Mendholz, the man up against whom I came in Switzerland in '18, he was very sore, but it was not a soreness to last ten or eleven years. If he had taken the first boat over from Germany after the Armistice and sought me out with a knife in his boot, I would have understood it."

Jupp raised his eyebrows.

"You were contra-espionage?"

"Yes. I was attached to the Intelligence. We fought an unofficial war against Germany in most of the neutral countries, particularly in Switzerland, where all good plotters went."

Jupp sat himself down in my ancestral chair and gazed dejectedly across the bare, highly-polished table at the trees beyond the lawn.

"Easy target. Room well-lit. Range, about fifty yards," he remarked. "And you don't know who'd try and do that to you?"

"Except Mendholz, about whom I'm very doubtful, nobody in the world."

He looked at me for a moment, and I noticed that the pupils of his eyes were so large that they almost obscured the whites. Rather kindly eyes, I thought them.

"How do you feel?" he asked. "Worried? Think there's a chance that this chap with the rifle may make another effort?"

I shrugged my shoulders.

"I shall keep in at night, and avoid sitting in lighted rooms with open windows. During the day, of course, I don't think there's much likelihood of an attempt although I think I shall carry a pistol in my pocket. Talking of windows, what made Hamish Page go near his? It was asking for trouble. He had been shot at once already, had seen me shot at, was as nervous as a cat about the whole thing, and had gone the length of sending for you."

Jupp shook his head slowly.

"If Hamish Page were here, one might discover that, and also if there was anyone in particular of whom he was nervous."

"It looks as though there might have been."

"It does. Which brings me to my chief reason for calling on you. I wonder if you could give me some kind of an idea of what Mr. Page was like? I've seen the body, I've seen that vast house of his, and I've seen members of his staff, but I really haven't established a contact with the man's personality. That is very important to me in the way I work."

I told him about the financier to the best of my ability, and after the manner in which I have already described him on an earlier page. He listened with careful if sombre attention, and when I had finished made comment.

"Not over attractive—and apparently of a sufficiently anxious disposition to be concerned about the safety of his skin, whether or not he had reason to suspect that some definite person wanted to murder him."

"He struck me as being like that—although perhaps not to the point of enlisting your aid to protect him, or rather to clear up the mystery. An ordinary village constable could have guarded him."

"At present," said Jupp, "this business is in a purely speculative state. This afternoon I am going to be practical, and visit the scene of the crime armed with all the resources of modern criminology—even to a magnifying-glass. Some time this morning Inspector English will get a wire from London about me, which ought to help me more than the magnifying-glass. I shall start level with the police. There are bound to be things they know which I might otherwise never learn. They were the first, you see."

"I wonder——" I began.

"You wonder if you could go with me this afternoon? I should like you to, Mr. Arden. You're the great white chief of this suffolk tribe, and to have you along with me would give me a *cachet* which, together with that telegram from London, will dispel the last of the Inspector's doubts about me."

His face lost for a moment a little of its grieved expression. He even smiled.

"It is very kind of you," I said. "Will you lunch with me here, and drive over afterwards?"

He thanked me, and saying that he wanted to hear the gossip in the bar of The Knife and Whistle, he departed through the french window.

I watched him go with a feeling that I had met a very pleasant, kindly and intelligent gentleman. At the same time it occurred to me to put through a trunk call to Bowers, at the Home Office, and ask him what George Jupp looked like. I did so, and had the satisfaction of having all suspicion put at rest. There could not be two people in the world who looked like that, and Bowers described the little man with characteristic accuracy and finish.

"He's a great connoisseur of wine," he added.

I thanked him, and gave Jupp a Montrachet 1911 with the lobster at lunch. The tears came into his eyes, and he all but wept with appreciation. He was George Jupp, all right, even if he took his pleasures sadly.

But between his visit to the bar of The Knife and Whistle and just before his return to the midday meal, Anita Skinner called on me, and a remarkable state she was in. She came about half-past twelve.

Outwardly, except for a restlessness of her thin hands, she was her usual well-groomed self, at ease with the world. Her expectant air, however, was missing, and her cold, faintly amused blue eyes were anxious. In the sunlight which poured into the library she was very blonde, and I wondered vaguely how she managed to look no more than her twenty-three years.

"John," she said, as she shook hands with me, "I'm in a hole."

I waited. It was a bad hole if she must come to me, or indeed to anybody, to pull her out.

"There's a letter of mine somewhere at Blyth Towers," she went on, speaking quickly and casually, but failing to disguise her anxiety, "—a letter they mustn't find."

"Yes?"

"Oh, don't be so brutally unconcerned!" she cried suddenly. "This is serious!"

"My dear child——"

"I'm not a child—and you're only forty-two," she retorted, "so don't pretend to be a grandfather. I've been foolish enough to tell you I love you—and I still do. I know you hate me . . . loathe me . . . but forget all that. I want your help."

If there was ever anything constant in Anita, it was her unexpectedness. She had never told me she loved me. It was the last thing in the world I had suspected. She had loved so many men in her short time: young men who were fascinated by her. And I, who was watching middle age approach, disliked her, as she rightly guessed! There was nothing about her which I found in the least attractive. Her ideals, if you could call them that, nauseated me.

"Your *help*!" she repeated.

"I will very gladly give it," I said quickly, "if I can."

"It isn't much that I want you to do. I can't go to the Towers and get the beastly thing myself—they'd be absolutely certain I killed the swine if I was caught searching for it. Particularly when they found it—and read it."

"This sounds perfectly ridiculous," I said. "What on earth can you have written to him that would start that kind of idea?"

She bit her red lips, and frowned.

"I wrote and said that I'd kill him rather than let him tell my father about what happened after the Hunt Ball—the last one, in February. And I believe I would have, if it had come to the point—if he'd told him. I—I—didn't, though. I didn't kill him."

Her eyes were eager for my belief.

"I never for a moment thought you had," I assured her. "And so there was something Page knew which you didn't want your father to know, and Page was using it as a lever of some kind?"

"He's been trying to get me to grant him the favour of my intimate company, and trying all he knows—even to this effort —this blackmail."

Her face was set and pale with hatred.

"Thank God he's dead!" she said. "He swore he'd *marry* me! Think of it!"

"Well, he can't now, and that's the end of it. There's no need to worry about him——"

"But there is! I'm telling you there is! There's that letter!"

"Even if they found it—and he may have destroyed it— you've got an alibi for that night. You went back to Inderswick with your father——"

"I could have got up any time during the night and gone over to Blyth Towers, shot him, and got back without a soul knowing. It's only a mile and a half, across the heath. Also there must be twenty different ·22 rifles lying around our place. You know what Father is. A firm will evolve some firearm, think it rather good, and send him a copy—like an author with a new book."

I was silent. What she said was perfectly true. She had had the means—and apparently quite a strong motive.

"Besides," she added a little desperately, "even if the police decided I didn't do it, Father would hear about that letter as soon as anybody. He'd be bound to. And he would want to know what it meant. I would have to tell him. He's as hard as bricks, that man. And cold. I don't think he's got a human feeling in him."

It was odd to hear Anita calling someone hard, cold and lacking in human feeling.

"And what you told him would—upset him?"

"He'd thrash me within an inch of life and fling me out of the house. 'Never-darken-my-door-again' sort of business. Antediluvian, and impossible; but nevertheless just what he'd do. You see, I got tightish after that Hunt Ball, and there were three men there, upstairs with me. . . . And I don't even remember their names. . . . Fun, you know, and all that. It hadn't happened before, and the notion occurred to me, in that particular state of spiritous elevation. . . . So now you know. I've told you, of all people. You, John . . . the one I want . . . and may yet have. Who knows?"

She laughed lightly, and seemed to have recovered, with confession, some of her normal poise. She inclined her head a little, gazed at me mockingly, and said:

"I've shocked the sociologist."

"You did that a long time ago. And Hamish Page knew about this adventure?"

"From the way he talked about it to me, I gathered he'd missed very little of it. He certainly offered to supply the men's names. I didn't want to know them, and told him so. He knew them, all right. John, you haven't the faintest notion what a devil that man was. It was torture to have to see him and pretend that I didn't mind. The night he was shot, when we all dined here with you, he kept looking at me as though I had done him some hurt. When he told us about the attempt to kill him I did not realise its significance. Otherwise I might have been in more of a panic than I was; I didn't want him to die with that letter lying about. Oh, what a fool I was to have written it at all! Get it back, John! For God's sake!"

"I'll try," I said. "I'm afraid, though, that if it's there to be found at all the police will have discovered it by now. It is thirty-six hours since the murder was known."

25

We were silent, and during the pause the door opened, and Jupp walked in. He did not see Anita immediately, for she had walked into the bay of the further window.

"The Knife and Whistle," he said, "is what you might term 'all agog.' D'you know a Miss Anita Skinner?"

"I do——"

But before I could add: "May I introduce you?" he went on:

"There's a rumour—and it seems to have a certain possibility of truth in it, judging by the authority of some lawyer's clerk from Southwold—that your murdered millionaire made a Will two months ago leaving that awful quantity of money to a Miss Anita Skinner——"

He was interrupted by a cry from the bay window.

Jupp raised his eyebrows in a thoroughly aggrieved fashion.

"Who the devil was that?"

"Miss Anita Skinner," I said.

"Ah!" remarked Jupp, and sat down suddenly on the nearest chair. "I suppose there's no chance she did it?"

"Very little," I said. "She seems to have had at least two motives, access to several ·22 rifles, freedom of movement during the night of the tenth, and a passionate nature."

"Too much like a murderess to be one?"

"Exactly. But the police may not see it that way."

"They seldom do."

"She won't make a good impression," I said.

"A very unpleasing young woman," he commented.

At that moment Jeames announced lunch; we passed on the Montrachet 1911, and murder was forgotten for an hour.

CHAPTER III

After lunch Jupp settled himself by my side for the short drive to Blyth Towers to meet Inspector English. We went through the park on to the main road.

"I've been wondering," he remarked.

26

"Yes?"

"Just whether she was acting—whether she knew that Page had made a Will in her favour."

"I don't believe she did. I saw her face. Surprise, anger, fear——"

"I saw her face too. Women are supposed to be good actresses. As a rule they are not—they're very bad ones—but when they're good they *are* good."

"Our Anita has never struck me as being the sort of girl who would bother to act."

"All women will bother to act if they have something to gain or something to conceal," announced Jupp with a gloom of extraordinary depth. So deep was it that I glanced at him quickly, a little startled, perhaps. Was he unhappily married? He read my thought in an uncanny way.

"Nearly was—once," he muttered into his chin. "Anyway, it's nonsense to say married men know more about women than the unmarried. Married can't see wood for the trees most of the time. Too far in it. . . . Miss Skinner's exit from your library was dramatic, to say the least of it, particularly in that laugh she sent floating up the stairs in her wake. Dramatic, if you see what I mean."

I thought for a moment.

"She had just been telling me, a moment before you came into the room, that she was in danger of being suspected."

"That would make a difference, of course. You mean she was already excited and distressed?"

"Yes, considerably."

Jupp did not speak for a few minutes.

"Care to tell me what is worrying her? Interests of justice, and so on?"

The way he put it, the tone of his voice, and the sudden sidelong flicker of his eyes, made refusal impossible. I decided that it could not increase Anita's danger to tell him; indeed, it might help her. So I told him the story.

He listened with what I recognised as his characteristic concentration, and did not say anything at the end.

"I forgot to point out to her," I added, "that she was one of the people who saw the attempt to shoot me—and that that happened within a few hours at most of Page's murder by precisely the same method and means. The open window, the rifle fitted with a silencer."

"The point is clear," he commented, "that, sitting at your dinner-table, she could not also let off a rifle at your head from a wood fifty yards away. That, of course, removes the personal implication, but not that of an accomplice. Did it strike you as odd that she did not see the value of having been present at that dinner-party?"

"Not at the time. It does now. By Jove!" I added softly.

He stared despondently at a herd of Jersey cows in a field we were passing.

"The person who made the attempts in each case supplied the alibi for the person who actually killed Hamish Page. In other words, it wouldn't be so impossible for the actual murderer to have sat at your dinner-table that night."

"Good God!" I said.

He smiled a trifle grimly.

"I love speculation theories—they're so bad for me."

"Who on earth of those four people—Professor Skinner, Lady Codrington, the Vicar, and Anita—is capable of working out a plot like that?" I asked.

"Well, how about Anita?"

"Then who is her accomplice? The sniping accomplice?"

"Some man who can do with three and a half millions. Someone she's in love with. Who's that waving at you?"

It was the Reverend Lionel Lake. He stepped off the path into the road and raised his blackthorn with an invitation to stop and have a little chat. Knowing this "little chat" habit of his, I proposed to drive past with a gesture explaining that we were in a terrible hurry, but Jupp said quickly:

"He was at that dinner-party of yours?"

"Yes."

"I would like to meet him."

I put on the brakes, and Jupp met the Reverend Lionel Lake.

The Vicar, who was never at a loss for something to say when there was nothing to talk about, inevitably became a perfect spate of words on those occasions when he really had a subject.

Oddly enough it was not the murder which occupied him this afternoon, save in as far as it affected another problem. Having said, "How d'you do?" to Mr. Jupp in a mechanical fashion very unlike his usual punctilious custom in such matters, he began:

"How fortunate indeed, Arden, that I should have met you! I was on my way to call on you. It is about the proposed gymkhana. We—the committee, that is—met this morning and discussed the whole matter of the chancel in the light of this most—ah—regrettable affair. It is now imperative that we should find a means of raising the sixteen thousand pounds. The agreements are signed and the work has actually commenced. Perhaps we were a trifle hasty; in fact, we did not allow for the unforeseen. But don't mistake me! The money was actually promised—the—ah—bill was to be sent to Mr. Page. His words to me three weeks ago were straightforward and clear. 'Vicar,' he said, 'I shall be only too pleased to help you in such a good cause. Send the bill in to me, and I'll see it's dealt with.' What could have been clearer?"

"Nothing," I said. "But surely his estate will pay it? Or his heirs?"

The Vicar sighed.

"I am no business man. I ought to have written to him and asked him to confirm his generosity in writing. But I did not. It was just a word spoken in his study at the Towers. No witnesses. Nothing. And as for the hope that his heir might carry out his wishes in the matter of our chancel, it is not one in which I can put any faith, Arden. I do not think——"

He paused, and I realised that, like ourselves, and probably everybody else in the neighbourhood by this time, he had heard the rumour about the millionaire's last Will and Testament. I also saw that, quite apart from the improbability of Anita spending any of those millions on his chancel, the mere idea of her acquiring all that money was enough to irritate him profoundly. He made a gesture which in a less pious gentleman might have been taken for one of disgust and contempt, and flung himself into the next phrase of his speech.

"We must stand on our own feet. I have told the committee that, and they see the wisdom of relying on no fortuitous circumstance to alter the position. We are in a serious predicament. Sixteen thousand pounds is far more than we can hope to raise by purely voluntary subscription in this small parish, where there are few well-to-do people. Thus we must fall back on bazaars, jumble-sales and so forth. The gymkhana next week must be much bigger than last year—better advertised and better attended. I have already written to the Eastern Counties Fairs Association, at Norwich, to have a real oldfashioned fair in conjunction with the sports. Now, Mr. Arden, our trouble is the matter of a site. The Common Field is too small, and rather far from the main road, the Vicarage garden is all right for bazaars and small affairs of that sort, and the common itself is undesirable—I doubt if legally we could charge admission. And so we decided, by unanimous vote, to approach you in the matter, and ask if you would consent to place the park of the Manor at the committee's disposal. It would be an ideal place: the natural beauty of the grounds, the ruins themselves—a sight which many people would come miles to see—and the park's accessibility both from the London road and the villages would be an inestimable advantage——"

He fixed me with round, determined eyes, and I knew that if I was to have any peace at all I would do well to consent, and consent immediately. I knew that it would take the park weeks to recover from the depredations of such an affair; it would take the outside staff months to clear up the last piece of orange peel.

"I think it could be arranged," I said, and to escape his protestations of gratitude prepared to drive on.

Jupp, who had been watching and listening with an air of vague misery which I realised concealed an acute observation of the Reverend Lionel, seemed ready also to get on to the Towers and his investigations. I shifted the gear out of neutral. At this moment the Vicar appeared to remember Hamish Page.

"Terrible! terrible!" he said. "Our poor friend! A dear friend! The wickedness! They're going to bury him at Saxmundham—he has a mother buried there, it seems."

I bade him good-bye and drove on, and for a moment one wondered whether the wickedness lay in the fact that the millionaire had been murdered, or in the decision to inter him at Saxmundham, and thus rob the Reverend Lionel of the best funeral of his career.

"He ought to have been a stockbroker," announced Jupp after a moment's silence.

It was a new and enlightening view of the Vicar.

"He has a knack of making people do what he wants them to do," I said.

"I don't believe I've ever seen a parson who more resembled the exaggerated parson of cheap fiction and the music-hall stage," he added.

"According to the gossip of the inhabitants of these parts, the Reverend Lionel doesn't always behave in the pious and sanctimonious manner which his speech and appearance might indicate."

"Don't tell me he's a wolf in sheep's clothing. I couldn't bear that."

"Not a wolf, just a gay Don Juan."

"Tut, tut," said Jupp, and transferred his interest from the Vicar to the countryside through which we were passing. Its wildness impressed him. We were within half a mile, perhaps, of the sea, and the stunted, twisted pine-trees spoke of the storms and winds against which they had fought for existence from the beginning of their days—the storms and winds which must inevitably conquer them. The moor, rising a little as it swept gently toward the fields and pasturage of the more sheltered inland, was brown and purple with passing heather. It was a deserted world, and it was a world which had not

31

changed since the days when Thomas Cromwell drove the monks from their rich possession of the coast, sacking their monasteries and razing their churches.

At the lodge gates of Blyth Towers there were two constables, and a number of gentlemen whom I saw to be newspaper reporters. These were arguing with the policeman. I explained to the constables, who recognised me, that Mr. Jupp was expected by Inspector English, and we were permitted to enter the drive after they had telephoned to the house. As I drove in I heard the reporters tearing at the word "Jupp" like dogs over a meaty bone. A camera clicked at the back of the car. We were to be brought before the notice of the public.

"If ghosts walk at all, they walk here," Jupp commented as we came in sight of the Towers. The big, sombre, grey granite house seemed cold and darkling, even in the sunlight of the afternoon.

"It is not as old as most of the buildings about here," I told him. "A hundred and fifty years, I suppose."

"Long enough to start a ghost or so. Suppose you find that letter, what are you going to do about it?"

The switch of subject startled me. His habit of speaking slowly, in the same tone of voice, made such changes seem more unexpected than might otherwise have been the case.

"Anita's letter, you mean? Hold on to it, and return it to her, I suppose. Discreetly."

"What about the police—and justice, and so on?"

"If I thought for a moment she had killed him it would be another matter, obviously; but——"

"But you don't *know* she didn't kill him."

"Good Lord, man! She's all sorts of a fool, and all sorts of a hard nut, but she isn't a murderess."

"She's a hysterical, highly-strung and probably morbid young woman of an unfortunate generation," stated Jupp, "a generation which was reared in its childhood in an atmosphere of strain—enormous strain, greater strain than we, who were grown up and better able to withstand it, realise. Food was scarce, and poor. It was never the food to rear children on.

You're a sociologist. Something of a psychologist as well. You know the effects of war on a community. The children——"

"But Anita Skinner," I said, "was brought up in America. Her mother took her there in '14, while the Professor got on with his armaments. He spent four of the busiest years of his life during the War, and he hadn't a moment to give to looking after a family. Guns, guns, guns—he breathed them. His wife was an American, and a nervous one. Europe looked rather a bloodthirsty place to be in, and she expected the Germans to invade England at any moment, particularly this coast, the nearest and handiest. She made a bee-line for Baltimore with her only daughter, who was then about ten, and stayed there until 1919, when she died of blood-poisoning a week before she was to return to England. Anita was sent home alone. She probably ate very good food indeed during those four years."

"All the same," said Jupp, unperturbed by this weakness in his theory, "she's hysterical."

He was right, of course. And apart from that, criminal history was not without several, if not many, instances of women no older than Anita, and apparently no less sane, who had committed murder. And with lesser motive and greater brutality.

As we turned into the open space of gravel in front of the house, Jupp asked me to point out the windows of Hamish Page's bedroom, and he sat for several moments after I had stopped the car gazing up at them in a kind of gloomy fascination. He also looked at the portion of the garden which lay opposite and beneath them.

Inspector English received Jupp with considerable and, I think, sincere cordiality. Jupp explained his position; he had been engaged by the dead man to solve the attempt on his life and prevent a further one, and now felt morally bound to do what little he could to help the police bring his murderer to justice. He did not for a moment suggest that it was anybody's job but the authorities', and he would not presume to suggest that they would be anything but successful. It was

33

merely that, in honour to the dead man's wish, he wanted to "be around," and naturally he would do nothing to obstruct the police. At the same time, if by any chance, or by reason of the fact that he had, as the Inspector knew, done a certain amount of criminal investigation work in the past, he came upon anything likely to be helpful to the inquiry, naturally he would at once take it to the Inspector, to make what use of it he cared.

The Inspector, I gathered, would be only too pleased. It seemed that he had heard of Mr. Jupp, and had required no telegrams from an influential source in London to assure him that it might be of considerable advantage to have Mr. Jupp "around." Mr. Jupp was a clever and quite ungreedy man, who might one day be discovered on the C.I.D. staff of Scotland Yard. It was conceivable. Also he always meant what he said. If in this case of Hamish Page he hit upon anything likely to help, he wouldn't keep it to himself. Bill English would get it, and it might do Bill English a bit of good. It behoved Bill English to make himself pleasant. Bill did.

"If you like," he said, "I can give you the story up to date, Mr. Jupp. I daresay you know some of it."

He glanced at me, decided that as the Squire of Eastblyth and Chairman of Trustees of the East Suffolk Police Pension Fund, I could be trusted, and went on:

"The police-surgeon, Dr. Allis, saw the body at eight-fifteen, and estimated that death had taken place between midnight and four o'clock in the morning. The body was found by the valet, Jackson, at about seven, or a few minutes past. It was lying under the window—I'll show you all that in a minute —in more or less of a heap. The window was open at the bottom, which was unusual, not to say exceptional, and we must assume that he opened it for some reason. He was shot through the head, almost exactly between the eyes, an inch and a quarter above them. I'd like to know *why* he opened the window and exposed himself like that, when he was already nervous on account of being shot at the evening before and seeing Mr. Arden, here, shot at that same night. Extraordinarily risky thing to do, to my way of thinking, and I

34

only wish he had called us in to give him protection. The two attempts would have justified it—more than justified it. Which reminds me, Mr. Arden; I think for your safety it would be as well if I put a man in the Manor garden of a night-time."

"Thank you, Inspector; I won't refuse. We all like to think we can look after ourselves, but on the whole I am sure I shall sleep easier for the thought that there's a hefty young policeman in the yard. Make him a hefty one, Inspector. As a matter of fact, I am hoping that Mr. Jupp will come and stay at the Manor while he is at Eastblyth. The Knife and Whistle isn't remarkable for the comforts of civilisation. There isn't even a bathroom."

"That is very kind of you," said Jupp. "I'll accept that invitation with gratitude. Mr. Arden, Inspector, has a cellar, and he has also a gift for characterisation. He knows everybody in this part of the world, and in the sort of way I find refreshing. He doesn't let his friendship for them interfere with his estimation of their morals and mentalities. That can be very useful to people like myself."

The Inspector nodded, and became thoughtful. He looked hard at Jupp.

"You don't think this is a *local* job, do you, Mr. Jupp?"

Jupp shrugged his shoulders.

"Let's hear what else you've discovered, besides a body."

The inspector considered for a moment.

"A whole lot—such a lot, in fact, that I don't know where to begin looking for the proper sort of line to follow. Mr. Page wasn't very well liked, you understand. I've spent this morning going through his papers with Mr. Snarlett, the Saxmundham solicitor who has dealt with Mr. Page's affairs since he came to these parts, and you've never seen such correspondence for a man to keep, let alone receive. He seems to have delighted in letters which told him just what the writers thought of him, and in quite a number of cases just what they'd like to do to him if they could get him alone in a quiet corner for five minutes. Threatening letters! I give you my word, some of 'em would put the chaps who wrote 'em in gaol for months!"

Jupp shook his head.

"Every millionaire, every public man, gets his share of them. I expect our Inspector English has them addressed to him sometimes."

This put the Inspector into the category of millionaires and public men. He smiled with grim satisfaction.

"Oh, I get them all right, but I don't take much notice of them. I never tie them up in yellow tape and keep them in a special drawer in my desk—come and meet Mr. Snarlett."

We went into Page's library on the ground floor, and there were introduced to the solicitor from Saxmundham, who was a tall, dry man with trembling, steel-rimmed pince-nez attached to him with a black ribbon, the weight of which seemed imminently likely to drag them off his nose. He was busy at the great desk in the middle of the room, and piles of papers lay in every direction. A clerk was occupied at a table, sorting a huge bundle. A six-foot safe, the existence of which I had never expected, stood revealed and open behind a door on the right-hand side of the big carved-stone fireplace. I looked at the mass of papers, and wondered where in it lay the letter Anita dared not let the police discover. If Hamish Page had made a hobby of collecting threatening letters, it would be unreasonable of him to have destroyed one written by the woman he hoped to marry. It would have been the choicest gem of the whole lot, and for that reason, perhaps, he had not put it with the main collection, but cherished it secretly in some hidden place. In which event it was not surprising that Mr. Snarlett and the Inspector had not yet come upon it, since they were eating the nearest piece of cake first, as it were. The search for a definite clue was as yet in its early stages, and there might be a chance for someone to find the Anita Skinner letter before the Inspector did, but, at the same time, when I considered the size of Blyth Towers, and the multitude of possible places in which it might be, the prospect was not too good.

"I'm going up to see the body," Jupp said. "Would you care to come?"

I shook my head.

"I'll come upstairs with you—but I think I'll let you conduct your examination alone."

Outside the library, as we went up the huge black marble staircase, Jupp remarked that if Inspector English believed in any complicity on the part of Anita Skinner, he was keeping it to himself.

"You don't think he's found that letter?" I asked.

"If it's as bad as the young woman says it is, and he had found it, he would be in a more active state of mind than he is in now. You're thinking you aren't going to have an easy job, finding it first?"

"I am thinking just that."

"And if you did find it, you would hand it over to us," said Jupp comfortably, and inquired of a policeman at the top of the stairs which would be Mr. Page's bedroom. He disappeared into it, and I continued along the passage to the small sitting-room in the south tower. I reflected that once again Jupp was right. It would be exceedingly foolish of me to withhold that letter in the unlikely event of my stumbling upon it, but not quite in the sense Jupp meant.

The small tower-room to which I now made my way alone, while Jupp satisfied himself about the details of Page's death, was a place the millionaire seldom used, but sometimes he had been known to lie down on the chesterfield after lunch or dinner, presumably to admire the excellent view of moor and sea until his ill-used digestive system allowed him to sleep for an hour. I had noticed the furniture on the one occasion, some months ago, he had taken me into the room, and I remembered a miniature Queen Anne walnut bureau in the corner by the east window. I had no particular reason for thinking Anita's letter might be in it, but it seemed as likely a place as any other if the desk and safe in the library had not yielded it.

I opened the door, which was unlocked, and stepped into the room. The bureau was still there, and I went over to it, which, as it happened, was as far as ever I got in my effort to save Anita from her letter-writing indiscretion.

37

She had committed a fresh one.

In that casual way one has of glancing out of the window of a room in which one has seldom if ever been, I looked across the broad lawn beyond the gravel space, and saw Anita standing under an oak tree. She was gazing at the house, and even at that distance, perhaps fifty yards or more, I was able to read her air of indecision.

I knew at once what she was doing, and why.

I ran out of the tower-room, down the stairs, and through the french windows of the billiard-room. More sedately I turned the corner of the house and crossed the lawn to her. She was surprised, and a trifle defiant.

"I oughtn't to have asked you to undertake what I did, this morning," she said.

"And because you doubted my ability to accomplish it," I went on, "you decided to have a try yourself. You're an idiot, Anita. You said yourself this morning that if you were discovered in such an attempt the suspicions of the police would become a certainty."

"*Don't* talk to me like a grandfather!" she cried angrily. "This house, this garden—all this—belongs to me, doesn't it? I have every right to come here if I want to—to enter the house——"

"Did you get here through the gate?" I asked, "or over the fence?"

She flushed.

"I *hate* you sometimes, John!"

"I'm thinking of the look of the thing," I said, "and also the fact that the Will has yet to be proved to the satisfaction of the Probate Court. Has Mr. Snarlett definitely informed you of the contents? Jupp said he had heard a rumour—that was all."

"It's true!" she snapped. "Six weeks ago Hamish Page told Father that he had made a Will naming me his sole legatee. When I got home after seeing you this morning Father said, in that silly dry way of his: 'Oh, by the way, I forgot. Page left you all his money.'"

I stared at her. Professor Skinner, then, had known about the destiny of those millions, if Page died. This was what one called "a development."

"So there!" said Anita, and turned to regard Blyth Towers with greedy, proprietorial eyes. She had hated Hamish Page, but she had forgotten that, and indecently soon, in contemplation of the great fortune he had bequeathed to her. Nothing in the world would have induced her to marry him, but equally true was it now that nothing in the world must keep her from her enjoyment of that fortune.

And this was the woman who had told me, with a frankness which had been less engaging than uncomfortable, that she loved me and would marry me yet!

"I'm going to look for that letter myself!" she said, and suddenly strode past me on to the open lawn. If Inspector English was near the library windows he would see her, but I could not, without immediately displaying what might later be shown to have been a disposition to take guilty sides with "the prisoner," make any move to restrain her. I called to her to come back into the trees, but she took no notice, and walked quickly toward the house. I shrugged my shoulders, and presently returned to the first floor, re-entering the house by the billiard-room, to find Jupp.

He was just coming out of Page's room, with a more sombre face than ever.

"No doubt about the way *that* happened," he said. "The Inspector's deductions cannot be got round on any point. Page opened that window, and somebody plugged him from the other side of the lawn. But I doubt if the medical evidence can do more than show that the range was not a short one —not a matter of inches, but of feet. Ten feet, fifty feet, a hundred. . . . Who knows?"

"In that case he could have been shot from *inside* the room. It's more than ten feet across, whichever way you measure it," I said.

"The line between the bullet's entry and the crack it made in the parietal bone shows that he was shot from a point several feet below the level on which he was standing," stated Jupp, and added unexpectedly: "How is Miss Skinner?"

"You saw her?"

"With you."

"I caught sight of her, and went out to urge her to go away," I explained. "I guessed, and rightly, that she had come to try to recover the letter for herself. She got in over the fence somewhere. She seems to have lost her head completely."

"You'll be arrested as an accessory after the fact if you go on being chivalrous to a murderess."

"I don't believe she's a murderess!" I exclaimed.

"Neither do I," said the amazing Jupp, and shook his head mournfully.

"I am certain she didn't know about the Will," I said, "even if her father did."

His pale eyes flickered with interest, and I told him about the Professor's casual recollection, thirty-six hours after the murder, that his daughter would inherit three and a half millions by reason of it.

"Curiouser and curiouser," said Jupp. "Here's the Inspector."

The Inspector came leaping up the stairs to meet us, his face a study of excitement and consternation.

"Mr. Jupp, Mr. Arden! *They've killed another one!* It's Lady Codrington! She's been found dead on the heath by Brooker's Mill! I've just had the phone message from East-blyth. I'm going over there now——"

"Any details?" asked Jupp.

"Shot through the head——" replied the Inspector. "Can you drive me over, Mr. Arden?" The three of us went out to the car together.

It was when we reached the gate, and the road, that I remembered Anita. If Anita avoided the library, where Mr. Snarlett was, she would have ample time and opportunity to conduct a search in every part of the house for that confounded letter of hers. Nobody would question her presence. I knew Anita. If she did not stroll about the place as though she owned it, which was nearly the case, at all events she would move confidently in it, as though she had authority and permission from the Inspector to do so. She was nothing if she was not an opportunist.

Well, it was nothing to do with me. Jupp had seen her in the garden; if he liked to warn the Inspector, he could. But he did not. Either he had forgotten the girl in the excitement of this news about Lady Codrington, or, like myself, he knew she had not killed Page and therefore attached no importance to the damning letter she was endeavouring to retrieve.

I drove fast along the narrow road across the heath which led to Brooker's Mill. The Inspector was the only one of us who spoke at all during those ten minutes, and at that it was but once, a short remark.

"Mark my words, gentlemen," he said, "this is going to be a very big case."

Neither Jupp nor myself was prepared to disagree with him. It was a very big case already.

CHAPTER IV

I was struck by the difference in the respective methods of Jupp and the Inspector in the matter of their investigations at the scene of the murder. The Inspector, having alighted from the car almost before I had brought it to a standstill, hurried towards the small group of people whose heads and shoulders were visible above the gorse bushes at a point some thirty yards from the road. Jupp, on the other hand, showed no immediate anxiety to view Lady Codrington's body. Instead, he paused to stare up at the ruins of Brooker's Mill, which stood on a slight hillock on the edge of the road on the opposite side to which the murdered woman lay. He strolled up the rise, and I accompanied him. We stood by a gap in the masonry and looked toward the place where the body was.

I understood the trend of Jupp's mind. He assumed that Lady Codrington had been killed in the same fashion as had

41

Hamish Page, and he was already looking for the place from which the marksman had fired the shot. The most obvious and reasonable concealment would be Brooker's Mill—assuming that the murderer was expecting her to appear conveniently in its immediate neighbourhood.

Jupp was merely doing now what the Inspector would do presently.

"This seems to be the range the fellow likes," he observed.

We walked round the segment of mill which faced toward the road and the body, and Jupp regarded the ground with intent eyes. After a moment, he said:

"Too hard for footprints, beloved to all criminal investigators, and not even a spent cartridge case to reward our bloodhounds. Either he took it away in the breech, if it wasn't an automatic ejector, or picked it up and put it safely in his pocket. The Scotland Yard microscopists are denied the chance to examine those subtle differences which can determine as surely as the finger-print system the relation or lack of relation between a cartridge case and the weapon from which its bullet may have been fired. Assuming, of course, that we ever got hold of the weapon. Remind me, Arden, will you, to ask the Inspector if he has got a list yet of the people in this neighbourhood who possess a .22 saloon or automatic rifle under Firearms Certificates? Let us go down and learn the worst. Presently I want you to tell me all about this unfortunate lady. She was, I believe, one of the famous dinner-party?"

"She was."

"You're upset—by this?" he asked suddenly as we made our way through the gorse bushes.

"Well, I am not going to pretend I am personally grieved. Lady Codrington and I never had much to do with one another. She was abroad a great deal, and did not enter into the life of the neighbourhood at all; if she had, I might have got to know her better. But naturally the news shocked me. After all, sudden death, you know. . . . And she had been dining in my house a couple of nights ago. Whatever kind of woman she was, death—murder—reduces things to another set of proportions."

"Quite," said Jupp. "She did not always behave herself?"

"She was what the Americans call a high-stepper, a hot momma."

We descended, and crossed the road into the gorse.

The group near the body consisted of the farm labourer who had made the discovery, his employer, John Jonathan, whom I knew, the police-constable they had summoned by telephone, and the Inspector, who said, with a grave face:

"Just the same—between the eyes. The fellow, whoever he is, must be a damned good marksman. As far as I can tell, the body has not been moved at all. This man here, who found it, says he just touched her shoulder, hoping but not believing that she was only asleep. The murder at the Towers has put the idea of dead bodies into people's minds, it seems. He says he knew she was dead the moment he set eyes on her."

"That's roight," said the farm-hand, his face flushed with the importance of the occasion.

"The sun," continued the Inspector, "has kept the back fairly warm, but I think it has been here like this for several hours. We can't be sure, of course, until Dr. Allis has seen it. I propose to telephone for him from Lady Codrington's house, leaving Goodall, here, in charge. There are one or two questions I want to ask this man." He turned to the farm-hand. "What time did you find the body?"

"Mebbe it was two o'clock, mebbe after——"

"How much after?"

"Mebbe half-past——"

"We'll say 'between two and half-past.' How did you come to make the discovery?"

"A walked round t' bush, an' seed she."

"What brought you to the bush—to this part of the heath?"

The man blushed.

"Rabbits, I dessay," remarked his employer caustically "Wastin' time."

The impeachment was not contradicted.

"All right," said the Inspector. "Did you see anyone in the neighbourhood?"

The man fidgeted with his ear. It was a very red ear, and pulling at it made it redder.

"I doan know," he said finally. "Mebbe Bill came by "

"Bill?"

"Postman," interpreted John Jonathan.

"On bike," said the man, glad to be rescued.

"No one else?"

He shook his head.

"Folks doan come this way much."

"I should say that was true," remarked Jupp, who had been surveying the empty landscape. "Why did *she* come this way?"

We drew away from the others, and the Inspector proceeded to make a careful search of Lady Codrington's hand-bag.

"Letter making an appointment?" asked Jupp.

"That's what I'm looking for, and there isn't a sign of one. As you say, this isn't the kind of place she would come by chance. She isn't dressed for walking. High-heeled shoes, grey crêpe-de-chine jumper and skirt, and a small hat—scarcely suitable attire for tramping about a moor in the sun. We may find a letter of that kind at her house. She wouldn't necessarily bring it with her if its purpose was merely to fix an appointment. She may have destroyed it, of course."

"Waste-paper basket; no fires in this weather," said Jupp. "She knew the person she was going to see—or thought she was going to see. She knew her murderer?"

"Hum," remarked the Inspector.

"Does one keep appointments with people one doesn't know?" Jupp asked, and went on talking to himself. "Depends on the nature of business to be transacted. Blackmailer? Not in this case, unless blackmail was used as the lever to get her here. Primary object, murder. Motive? Ah! Search, search, search—poke and pry and ask questions. Questions, questions. Where's the motive? Arden, why should anybody want to kill Lady Codrington?"

"Good Lord! Who knows?" I exclaimed. "It might be a *crime passionel*. Revenge, jealousy, anything."

"I was asking for scandal."

"Oh, I see. That's difficult; but not because there isn't any."

"Too much?"

"That's the way of it, to my idea. She enjoys the grand passion. Makes a hobby of it."

"Like Anita being too much of a murderess, Lady Codrington is too much of a victim."

"Anita?" said the Inspector sharply. "You mean Anita Skinner?"

Jupp blinked, for he had been ruminating aloud and using me as a kind of chorus.

"Anita Skinner is a young woman I'm keeping my eye on," added the Inspector. "If she hadn't been present at the dinner when the attempt was made on Mr. Arden, I should have been rather inclined to inquire into her movements later that night, when Mr. Page was killed. In any case, I think I shall."

Jupp rubbed his hands.

"A suspect, Inspector?"

The Inspector looked cautiously about him.

"Between ourselves, gentlemen, and in the strictest confidence, Mr. Page made a Will a few weeks ago leaving all his money to Miss Skinner. *All* of it!"

"Dear me," muttered Jupp, gazing at the Inspector in alarm. "All of it?"

"Every penny of those millions——"

I saw that Jupp did not consider it necessary to inform the Inspector that the whole countryside knew about the Will.

"He must have been very fond of her," he commented.

"He was going to marry her."

"Oh, well, that explains it, doesn't it?"

"If I thought that young lady was as wicked as everybody says she is, I wouldn't put it past her to hurry up the process of inheritance," said the Inspector. "But it wouldn't be exactly necessary, since she was going to marry the money. That was going to bring her to it quick enough."

I realised that he had not found Anita's threatening letter, and I further realised that if he ever did he would become morally certain that she had had something to do with the murder of the millionaire. As Jupp had earlier suggested, the police would be more than inclined to consider her guilty if they knew so much as we did, in spite of the fact that she had been present at the attempt on me, and therefore could not have been the person to make it. They would, again as Jupp had suggested, begin to look for her accomplice.

Then the Inspector dropped a remark which did not startle me but caused Jupp to look up quickly. It came so swiftly at the heels of my thought about Anita's possible accomplice as to be almost uncanny.

"I think that secretary of the Professor's is sweet on her," said the Inspector.

"Blake!" I said. "But Blake——"

"Yes?" inquired the Inspector, encouragingly.

I had been about to protest, like Anita, that Blake was the last young man in the world to commit murder to gain money. He had many peculiar and high-minded notions, and he always showed a strong disposition whenever he met me to argue on subjects about which I might be supposed as a sociologist to know something. One of them was this business of personal property. According to James Blake, nobody ought to possess anything. Possession, he claimed, stimulated the acquisitive instinct, and the acquisitive instinct stifled the soul quicker than dipsomania. It was perhaps odd, when one came to think of it, to find him helping an international expert in armament to perfect methods whereby human beings might slaughter one another. But if he was in love with Anita, that might explain the inconsistency. I realised that even if the police were to agree that he was not the actual murderer for profit, they would not necessarily agree that he could not have become one in some mood of despera-tion aroused by Anita. Theoretically, and even practically, he could have killed Hamish Page. Ethically it seemed un-likely. The police, however, seldom concerned themselves with ethics. I saw that if they learnt how badly Anita had hated Page, how determined she had been never to marry him, and that she had written a letter swearing to kill him if he went to her father with the story of the Hunt Ball, they would be in no doubt as to the direction their inquiry should take. Anita's alibi in being present when the attempt was made on me would not save her from the noose as an accessory before and after the fact. Unless James Blake also had an alibi for the night of the tenth; he slept in a room above the big workshop in the Professor's grounds, some distance from the house. Slept there alone. He could have got up at any time he chose during the night, walked across to the Towers, shot the millionaire with one of several ·22 rifles Anita had admitted were lying about the Professor's establishment, probably in the workshop, and returned to bed unseen and unheard.

Personally it had never occurred to me that he was in love with Anita, but the Inspector seemed to have an inkling that such was the case. It was, of course, conceivable. Anita was attractive in the way that a diamond is attractive. She glittered, and her hardness was not the first thing which one saw. Blake might have fallen for her, in spite of her selfishness and moral instability. I liked him, and now suspicion was gathering against him.

While my mind had been occupied with these things, the Inspector and Jupp had been carrying out a systematic but unproductive examination of the ground near Lady Codrington's body, and when they had finished we moved off toward the car, the Inspector saying:

"Would you be so kind as to drive us to the poor lady's house, Mr. Arden?"

"Willingly."

As we got into the car I made a tentative remark.

"This second murder removes Miss Skinner from the possibility of having anything to do with the first—with either of them—don't you think?"

"Why?" asked Jupp.

"Well, I mean——"

"Suppose Lady Codrington knew something about Mr. Page's murder," said the Inspector. "Suppose she *saw* the person or persons at their guilty work. *Suppose she was killed because she knew too much.* What then?"

"Exactly," remarked Jupp. "One murder is so inclined to necessitate another."

"And sometimes a third," said the Inspector cheerfully.

"You mean *mine*?" I asked.

The change in his face was almost laughable.

"They did try, you know," I added.

Jupp came to the rescue.

"Continuing your theory of Anita Skinner's complicity, aided by an accomplice who was not present at the dinner-party, the attempt on Arden might be no more than an effort to create an alibi for her."

"You've suggested that before," I said.

"Ah!" cried the Inspector. "Are we on the same trail, Mr. Jupp?"

Jupp shrugged his shoulders, and fell into a gloomy silence, and I saw that I had not improved matters as far as Anita was concerned. Indeed, I had made them worse by giving the Inspector the feeling that the great Jupp agreed with his theorising. He would transfer it into practice, and before I knew what was happening, Anita and James Blake might come near to being charged with the double murder. Anita might come out of such an ordeal unhurt, for spiritually she had the hide of a pachyderm, but James Blake was more sensitively constituted. It might smash him badly. Anita didn't matter, but Blake was worth preserving.

I hoped profoundly that Page had destroyed Anita's letter. She had been right in calling it "damning."

Suddenly Jupp spoke.

"In the meantime, there's someone stalking about the neighbourhood with a ·22 rifle fitted with a silencer. Does he make a nick in the butt for each killing? Which reminds me. If this is local, you've got the Southwold police records of Firearms Certificates. You might come upon something useful in them."

"I'll have a man go through them at once," said the Inspector. "Meanwhile, I'm going to fill this neighbourhood with policemen—an organised patrol on a big scale. . . . I'm not going to risk anything——"

Jupp nodded approvingly, and turned to me.

We drove on, and came at length to "Four Ways," the small Elizabethan farmhouse at the cross-roads outside East-blyth, which Sir John Codrington had bought and restored a year before his death in 1922. His widow had continued to live there for the last seven years, whenever, that is to say, she was neither roaming the Continent on romantic endeavours nor occupying a prominent place in that somewhat exotic circle of Russian-tea drinking, would-be *literati* which has recently moved from Chelsea to the lower heights of Hampstead. Lady Codrington, as I explained to Jupp, was an authoress. At least three heavy-papered volumes of hers had been published in English by the Sappho Press, a firm which found Paris a less critical city than London regarding the works it published in the names of Art and Realism. The Home Office, being of the opinion that if these showed Art they also showed Realism of the starkest kind, persistently refused to permit their import into the British Isles. This attitude was vilified on the lower heights of Hampstead, but deplored by the rest of the country, which did not know, of course, what it was missing.

The house was tranquil, for no word had yet come to it of the tragedy; the police had kept John Jonathan and his farm hand to themselves, and the village had still to hear the terrifying news.

The maid, Annie Stannard, who opened the door to us was excited and confused at the sight of Inspector English, for obviously his visit had something to do with the murder at Blyth Towers.

"M'lady's not in," she said. "She was comin' in to lunch, but I think she's over at the Professor's."

The Inspector told her that that didn't matter, and in the meantime there were one or two questions he wanted to ask. He did not tell her what had happened to her mistress, and in that he was wise if he wanted to get any sense out of her. He assumed, rightly, that Annie Stannard rather than the cook would be able to give him the kind of information for which he was looking.

Annie took us into the small sitting-room off the hall—the room, indeed, where Lady Codrington had written *Behold! Love!* and the others of that kind—and we sat down. The Inspector, despite tradition, did not take out a note-book. He began at once with a series of quick questions.

"Everything has been going along here as usual, Annie?"

"Yes, sir. I think so. About the same. Except, of course, since Mr. Page was—murdered." She looked apprehensively at us.

"Oh? Things have been different since then?"

"M'lady was upset, very upset. It was through her that he came to Eastblyth. She helped him with the Towers—decorating, curtains, and that. M'lady is very good at curtains. Those blue ones everybody admires so at the Towers she——"

"Never mind about the curtains. When did your mistress hear about Mr. Page's death?"

"Why, when the Vicar told her—it would be about ten o'clock yesterday morning. The morning after M'lady went to dinner at the Manor, that was."

"The Vicar came to tell her? She was quite unprepared for the news?"

"Oh yes. And we had an awful time with her. She's very sensitive, is M'lady. Things upset her something terrible. A dog barking 'll give her a headache, and when she's at her writing nothing can be too quiet in the house. The Vicar was quite frightened, the way she took on. Smellin' salts, and asperin, and what not. They was great friends."

"I see. Tell me, Annie. Lady Codrington went out this morning. What time was that?"

"Half-past eight, sir."

"Rather early, wasn't it?"

"A bit, p'r'aps; but it was a fine day."

"What time does she usually get up?"

"Ten, sometimes eleven. Sometimes seven o'clock, when she's writin' a lot."

"She doesn't often go out as early as half-past eight?"

"No-o. I suppose she doesn't. But, then, there's lots of things she does she doesn't do usual, you see. She's like that, M'lady is. It's the artistic temperature, Cook says."

"Had she had breakfast before she went out?"

"Coffee and a piece of toast—the same as usual, in her room."

"Did she say where she was going?"

"No, sir."

"Had the post come before she left?"

"No, sir, that doesn't get here till half-past nine, sometimes nearly ten. It's all accordin' to the weather. Cook says if Bill, that's the postman—I beg your pardon, sir——"

"Think carefully now, Annie, before you answer this question. Did your mistress receive any message, any letter, or any telephone call last night or first thing this morning?"

"Message, sir?" said the girl doubtfully. "I don't remember no message. There was a note from the Vicarage about nine o'clock last evening, and there was a telephone call from Southwold, from the garidge what is getting M'lady the new car. Somethin' about the insurance, I think it was."

"Only a note from the Vicarage," said the Inspector. "Nothing else?" He turned to Jupp. "I'm assuming that this second business is in direct relation to the first. If there *was* a decoy message, it would have come within the last twenty-four hours."

"That's sound," agreed Jupp.

I asked a question of Annie, who was gazing from one detective to the other in vague alarm.

"Who brought the note from the Vicarage?"

"It came in at the letter-box, sir. Oh, sir, has—has somethin' *happened*?"

The Inspector shepherded her out of the room, and spoke

to her in the passage. We heard a cry of dismay, a burst of tears, and a scurry to tell "Cook." The Inspector returned with a wry face, and picking up the telephone, called up Dr. Allis to tell him that there was another body for his examination.

While he was talking to him, Jupp walked over to the writing-table in the window. A moment later he dived into the waste-paper basket, and picked out a screw of paper, which he smoothed. He glanced at it, went across to the Inspector, and held it so that he could read it while he was telephoning.

It had the effect of cutting short Dr. Allis' questions, for the Inspector put the receiver on the hook, and reached out his hand.

"It's the one!" he exclaimed. "But it's signed 'Lionel'; and it's on the Vicarage notepaper. Lionel! that's—that's—the Vicar! It's ridiculous!"

Jupp shrugged his thin shoulders.

"It may be, but it certainly explains why Lady Codrington went to Brooker's Mill at half-past eight this morning."

"Where was it?"

"In the waste-paper basket."

"But, good heavens, the Vicar couldn't have shot her!" The Inspector glared at the note, and read: "'Dear Katherine. Will you meet me at Brooker's Mill at eight-thirty to-morrow morning? I must talk to you, and alone. We shall be undisturbed there at that hour. Yours—Lionel.'"

"May I see the handwriting?" I asked. "I know the Vicar's quite well."

He showed it to me.

"It *looks* like his," I ventured. "I agree with you that he is scarcely the person to shoot Lady Codrington. He's too short-sighted for one thing. But he may be able to tell you what he wanted to talk to her about, and he may have seen something of the murderer."

"The Vicar," said the Inspector, "is the very next person I'm going to see."

But the Vicar wasn't. At that moment the telephone rang,

and the Inspector seized the instrument. After a moment he said in a tone of surprise:

"Yes, Mr. Snarlett, this is Inspector English. How did you know I was here? Oh, Allis—of course. Yes, I've just been talking to him. Yes, Lady Codrington. It's appalling, isn't it? *What?*"

We watched his face, and the excitement which spread over it as he listened to what the lawyer had to say. I realised, then, what it was all about. The Inspector nodded to himself once or twice, and finally said incisively:

"Quite right! Yes. Don't let her go—on no account whatever. Use force if you have to, but DON'T LET HER LEAVE THAT HOUSE! Yes. I'm coming at once. Good-bye!"

He slammed down the receiver.

"Something definite at last!" he cried. "Snarlett has caught the Skinner girl rummaging about in a bureau at the Towers! She got in somehow, I suppose, and escaped notice. It's a big house. But this is the important thing! In that bureau Snarlett has found a letter in which the writer threatens to kill Hamish Page! Yes, I know you'll say there are lots of those. There are. But this one was written by—whom do you think?"

Jupp shook his head, and I said nothing, although we both knew. Perhaps we did not like to rob the Inspector of his triumph.

"*Anita Skinner!*" he announced, and seized his hat from the chair. "Thank Heavens Snarlett came upon her before she got hold of it! I'm going over there now. . . . The car again, Mr. Arden, if I may trouble you."

"Certainly," I said, and realised, as I drove the two detectives back to Blyth Towers, that I was about to witness a dramatic scene. The Inspector believed that he was going to interview a murderess. Jupp might be thinking the same thing, but with Jupp one never knew. He slouched in the seat at my side, his hat brim pulled over his eyes, and considered his sombre, secret thoughts.

It was as we were passing through Eastblyth village that

I noticed the stranger with the red beard standing in the doorway of The Knife and Whistle, and at the time put him down as one of the newspaper men. The momentary picture of him remained in my mind however, in an odd way, and later that afternoon I saw him again.

And remembered him.

CHAPTER V

I SHALL never forget the grimness of the atmosphere in the library of Blyth Towers when the three of us walked into it: the Inspector, Jupp and myself. A high, vaulted room, dark with books and tall, narrow, stained-glass windows, it had a gloomy air on the brightest day. But that afternoon, when the minds and emotions of the people in it were occupied with the weight of two mysterious murders, it was gloomy indeed. Suspicion was pointing an accusing finger at the girl Anita, who lay in a large leather armchair by the stone fireplace, her poise expressive of an ease we knew she could not feel, and watched the faces of us all, watched Snarlett, the lawyer, who had found her searching the Queen Anne bureau in the sitting-room upstairs. Snarlett, I realised, was the man who had helped Hamish Page to put his Will into legal form, and who knew, therefore, like ourselves, that Anita was the heiress. Did he, in common with Inspector English, believe she had committed murder to expedite her inheritance? There was something predatory about his long, black, bony figure as he stood near the armchair, his hands clasped behind his back like folded wings, and his pince-nez drooping toward the end of his curved nose. There was a police constable just inside the door, and he also was keeping an eye on Anita Skinner, but in a more stolid fashion. The lawyer's clerk was still sorting papers at the table in the corner.

Into this scene the Inspector broke with a quiet, purposeful bustle.

"Mr. Snarlett," he said, "have you anything of material importance to add to what you told me over the telephone?"

"I don't think so. Miss Skinner——"

Anita cut short the lawyer.

"This silly old idiot," she said, "has dared to keep me here against my will! He is quite mad, of course."

The Inspector stood in front of her.

"We feel we cannot permit you to trespass on premises which do not belong to you, and thereon attempt to obstruct the police in the execution of their duty," he stated sternly, "and that is a serious criminal offence."

"What is this nonsense about the Towers not belonging to me? Will you please tell me if Hamish Page has left it to me or not?" Anita was giving a very creditable performance of a young woman whose just rights are being disregarded.

"Whatever may be the contents of Mr. Page's Will," replied Mr. Snarlett, "it has not yet been admitted for probate. Until it becomes effective by order of the Probate Court it can have no legal value. This house is *not* yours."

"Miss Skinner," interposed the Inspector, "I understand that you made your way in here and proceeded to open and search a certain desk. For what were you looking?"

Anita scowled, and kicked at the fringe of a Persian rug. She looked at me, and I nodded. She could gain nothing now except by absolute frankness.

"A letter," she said sulkily.

Snarlett handed the Inspector a sheet of notepaper, which he read quickly.

"I see," he remarked, and held it by one corner in front of Anita. "Is this the letter for which you were looking?"

"Yes."

"Can you tell me how you came to write it?"

"No!" cried Anita. "I can't! I won't! If you think I shot the beast, you were never so wrong in your life!"

"On the face of the facts," pursued the Inspector, "and perhaps going into them more deeply, I don't see how I can regard you as entirely innocent. Here is a plain statement of an intention to kill. It is signed by you, and it is addressed to the deceased. Would you like me to read it to you?"

"No! I wish to God I had never written the wretched thing!"

"Very well, then, make up your mind that the only hope you have of lifting the suspicion which must inevitably fall on you in view of the circumstances is to tell us the whole story."

"Damn!" said Anita, and got out of the chair. She looked at her finger tips for a moment.

"He was blackmailing me," she said, after a moment.

"I think it might be better," interrupted the Inspector, "if we had this in the form of a statement. It will save a lot of bother."

"If I don't care to make a statement, I needn't," she remarked, and eyed the policeman coldly. "I can ask for legal advice, and legal advice would almost certainly say 'Keep your mouth shut.'"

"Not necessarily," I said. "In fact it would probably agree with the Inspector. To keep silent would have one certain effect: it would add to the suspicion with which every thinking person who knows the facts must view your part in this business."

"I had no part in it! You know that, John!"

"In the crime, of course not. I know that. But I also know that you have behaved foolishly since, and that you are in no position to say: 'Believe what you like—I don't care.' Do you want to get yourself arrested?"

The Inspector glanced approvingly at me; apparently I was saying what officially he could not say but wanted to.

"Oh, all right."

English nodded to the constable, who sat down at the desk, and wrote down what Anita said.

In substance it was more or less what she had told me earlier in the day. She told the Inspector of Hamish Page's method of trying to get her to marry him—his blackmailing, his threatening to go to her father with the story of her indiscretion after the Hunt Ball. She told him of her desperation at finding herself in such a very cleft stick, and how in this mood she had written the threatening letter. She had not known until after Page's death that he had made a Will in her favour.

"Who told you that he had?"

"That man there," said Anita, and pointed to Jupp, "and also my father, afterwards."

The Inspector jumped.

"*Jupp!* How——"

I stepped forward, and said quickly:

"Miss Skinner was at my house this morning, Inspector, when Jupp came in at lunch-time. Before he realised Miss Skinner was in the room, and before he realised that she was Miss Skinner at all, he mentioned that he had heard a rumour at The Knife and Whistle about Page having left all his money to a Miss Skinner, and wanted to know if I knew her. She heard what he said, and appeared to be very upset at the news. I think she realised that things might look black against her."

"Oh?" said the Inspector suspiciously. "So she was upset. What did she say?"

"As far as I remember, it was something to the effect that she wished he hadn't—at all events, she cried out, and ran down the stairs and out of the house without waiting to say good-bye. She was definitely perturbed. Unless she was acting she had not heard before that moment that Page had made her his legatee."

"Why didn't you tell me all this before?" English demanded.

"Until this minute it had not struck me as being pertinent to the situation," I replied.

"Hum," he said, and turned to Anita again.

Jupp, who had successfully effaced himself during the last few minutes by wandering along the bookshelves, now returned to the neighbourhood of the fireplace, and had an admirably close view of Anita's face when the Inspector asked her the next question, and I wondered whether Jupp had been expecting him to put it. The Inspector read the statement over to himself, gave it back to the constable, and faced the girl again.

"Until the time of Mr. Page's death, Miss Skinner, you kept this blackmailing business to yourself? You did not confide in anybody?"

"Why should I?" she snapped quickly.

"People say that 'a trouble shared is a trouble halved.' It would be not unlikely for a young lady, finding herself in the predicament in which you found yourself, to go to a friend for help and advice. Tell me, was there in this case some such friend?"

Anita opened her mouth to say, "No," and then closed it; closed it tightly. Her expression changed for an instant, and as quickly resumed its former wariness. None of us missed that change, and although I, and perhaps Jupp with me, read it as resulting from some sudden mental illumination, I think the Inspector saw it only as one of determination not to mention the name of someone to whom she had confessed the importunity of Hamish Page—before Hamish Page's death.

Jupp and I saw it as that also, but where the Inspector seemed to make a mistake was in assuming that Anita was shielding an accomplice. Actually I was ready to believe that she was shielding someone who, for all she knew, *might* have committed the murder to save her from the blackmail of Hamish Page.

The Inspector repeated his question with gentle insistency.

"Was there someone in whom you confided?"

"No," said Anita in a low voice, and for a moment there was a silence which the Inspector's voice broke as with a startling noise, although he did not raise it above the normal tone of conversation.

"Is that your considered answer?"

"It is," she said, and turned on him with sudden savagery. "Must you poke and pry and question? *Must* you? Can't you leave people alone? Oh, you're loathsome, loathsome!"

"It's my job to protect the community," he stated, and then sprang the trap: "There is a murderer at large. Some-one who has killed—twice!"

Anita drew in her breath with a sharp cry.

"*Twice?*"

He said nothing, and in mingled horror and apprehension she stared first at him and then at Jupp and myself. I came nearer to feeling sympathy for her at that moment than I had ever come; there was a quality of terror in her eyes which I found hard to meet. Her lips moved.

"Who—who else has—has——? *Not*——!"

But she stopped there, as though fearful of committing herself, or someone for whom she feared.

"Some time early to-day, Miss Skinner," said the Inspector slowly, "the man who killed Hamish Page shot Lady Katherine Codrington—shot her dead on a lonely heath!"

Nothing in all that surprising day seemed afterwards so startling as the instant relief with which Anita relaxed the tension of her anxiety. She sighed, and threw herself into the armchair, to tuck her feet under her and smile—actually smile.

"Ah," she said. "Poor Katherine. . . . I'm so sorry."

The Inspector's brows came together, and I saw how badly she had shaken him. He scarcely noticed her callous acceptance of Lady Codrington's murder, her vague, polite regret. He was asking himself the obvious and apparently unanswerable question which both Jupp and I were asking:

Of whose murder had she been expecting to hear, that she should be so instantly relieved to learn that it was merely Lady Codrington who had been shot dead on a lonely heath?

The Inspector was at a loss. He stroked his chin and glared at Anita, who was helping herself to a cigarette from a tortoiseshell case she had taken from the pocket of her tweed coat. She seemed to have recovered herself in an astonishing way. It looked as though she saw her own salvation in this second murder, and not only her own, but also that of the person whom she was afraid was responsible for the first. "All right," said her attitude now, "go find a motive which would induce Anita Skinner to murder Lady Codrington. Or want her murdered."

"I must ask you," said the Inspector finally, "to keep yourself at our disposal in the further inquiries which we propose to make. If you would sign this statement, that will be all I require of you at the moment."

She grinned a little; she knew that she had emerged from a peculiarly awkward situation with greater success than she might have done. Suspicion still hung heavily above her head in the form of the traditional cloud, but it had not fallen upon her. Anxiety on one account or another remained with her, but she could cope with it, fight it and perhaps conquer it altogether. In the meantime, she was free to come and go, provided she did not go further than the immediate eye of the Law could see.

She nodded to us, and lounged unhurriedly out of the library, and I would have found it hard at that moment to explain precisely how she had averted the Inspector's handcuffs; unless it was that she had shown herself secure in spirit at a moment when materially all her defences had been broken down.

Into the middle of the silence which fell upon us at her exit Jupp dropped one of his Jupp-like remarks.

"The more of a bad name you give that dog the better she likes it."

"She knows something!" exploded the Inspector. "I'm absolutely sure of it!"

"Women are queer," said Jupp. "They can *think* they know something, and behave as though they really knew it, and beat people like you and me, Inspector, when it comes to finding out something they would like to know."

"Meaning?" asked the Inspector.

"She'll now go and badger the life out of Mr. James Blake, to discover if he killed Hamish Page, and whether Lady Codrington saw him do it, and was that why he killed her too? And when Mr. James Blake denies knowledge of the whole business, she'll be angry about nothing in particular and secretly relieved, because she will have found out what she wanted to know."

"And what was that?"

"That Mr. James Blake murdered neither of them."

"Tchah!" muttered the Inspector irritably.

CHAPTER VI

Marchison, the Towers butler, served us tea in the library, and during the interval it formed, the Inspector seemed to realise suddenly how little information had come to him from outside sources. He explained that in most criminal cases the police relied upon the "common informer" to a considerable extent, if not for direct evidence, at least for angles from which profitable inquiry might be conducted. In nearly every murder case somebody knew something which they were in a hurry to tell the police. So far, not a soul had come forward with a story of this person or that being seen a-prowl with a rifle under his arm. It was true that the news of Lady Codrington's murder had not yet become general, but apart from that there had been three separate occasions when the murderer had moved about the countryside with his weapon.

"Not counting the Vicar," the Inspector reassured himself, "there is a bigger chance the fellow was seen by someone before or after he shot Lady Codrington, for the simple reason he was moving in daylight, even if it was early. But quite a lot of people are a-stir in the country by eight o'clock—farmhands going to work, the postman, and so forth."

"That's true enough," Jupp agreed, "if he is the sort of man to have allowed himself to be seen."

"He can't be infallible."

"No. But doesn't it strike you that he is very deliberate? There's nothing of the impulsive murderer about him—the type who kills on the spur of the moment and finds that he has a whole lot of unforeseen circumstances to deal with before he can escape. And that is, after all, the type of which the murdering classes are largely composed, and which presents no difficulty where you and I are concerned, Inspector."

"That's all very true. I'm simply looking at the trouble anyone would have in carrying a ·22 rifle about the place without it being noticed. If it were a knife or a pistol it would be another matter."

"I've been wondering where the theory first started that it *is* a rifle," commented Jupp.

We both looked at him, and Snarlett nodded slowly.

"No one has seen the weapon," he remarked.

"It was Professor Skinner's idea, at the dinner," I said. "I think he assumed that it must be a rifle."

"Why?" persisted Jupp. "When there is such a thing as a ·22 pistol?"

"Is it as accurate?" I asked.

"That's a pertinent observation. It is not. Use a silencer and it becomes even less accurate. Mind you, the bullet which was fired at you missed. There was nothing to show that that was due either to bad shooting, deliberate intention or inaccuracy of weapon. I still don't see why Professor Skinner jumped to the conclusion that it was a rifle. Personally, in view of the similarity of the wounds in the two actual killings, I am inclined to the rifle theory."

"The Professor is an expert on firearms," I suggested lamely.

"Is he also a good rifle shot?" asked Jupp.

The Inspector stared at him.

"But he was at the dinner-party——"

"So was his daughter——"

"But she had motive and plenty for killing Page—to say nothing of an accomplice to do the actual work if she didn't like it."

"True. I'd forgotten," said Jupp gloomily.

The Inspector still stared at him, while the lawyer stroked a lantern jaw and stared also. I thought I knew what Jupp was getting at. He meant them to see that, in his humble opinion, it was almost as reasonable to suspect the Professor as any one of the three that remained of the five who had dined with me, not necessarily because he thought them all innocent, but because he refused to believe that Anita was guilty either in knowledge or in act. The interview with her which had just been concluded had dispelled any suspicion he may have had, whatever the Inspector or anybody else might care to think. As politely as possible he was telling the Inspector that he was on the wrong track.

Whether that worthy and painstaking man realised this, I do not know, and whether if he did he placed any value on it, I also do not know, but at all events he appeared to remain puzzled by Jupp, reluctant to disregard him altogether, Jupp's reputation being such as forbade anything so foolish, but equally cautious lest Jupp's obscure methods of deduction lead him into omitting some practical step in the investigation. No less politely, his air suggested that Jupp was entitled to his own opinion, but that for himself he preferred his own way of working things out. Motive and opportunity, behaviour and the existence of a possible accomplice—all these pointed toward Anita Skinner, and he was content to bear that fact clearly in mind. As in the Croydon arsenic case, when the police had their theory from the beginning, thus in this affair it was only a matter of finding proof. It would come; he was confident of that.

And some was to be provided by the Reverend Lionel Lake, who, hearing about the second murder from Tom Ladd, the boat-builder and undertaker, jumped on to a bicycle and hurried to the Towers in a twitter of nervousness.

"Saves us another motor drive, at all events," observed the Inspector, who had just finished a lengthy telephone conversation with his headquarters, and with the Chief Constable, when the Vicar was announced. "This," he added, "is where I find something to set my teeth in."

The Reverend Lionel Lake strode into the library, darted up to the Inspector, and cried:

"This terrible, terrible state of affairs *must* end, sir! Something must be done! That poor, dear lady. . . . It does not bear thinking about! Who next? people are asking. And upon my soul can you blame them? Is there one of us who does not fear to step out of the shelter of our walls lest an assassin's bullet pierce our brain? The village is in a state of panic! The gentry are demanding that the authorities take full and immediate measures to protect the community from danger. It is an outrageous thing, sir, that in this twentieth century men and women should be struck down by an unseen hand, and the perpetrator go free and unapprehended!"

He paused to mop his face with a yellow bandana handkerchief while the Inspector calmed him.

"Everything is being done, Mr. Lake, that can be done. Nobody realises better than I the gravity of the situation, and I can assure you that we are making adequate provision to meet it. I have already arranged for protection: twenty-five men are arriving at Eastblyth to-night, and there will be a systematic patrol in operation from eight o'clock onwards through every twenty-four hours. I do not anticipate any further—er—trouble."

"Trouble," muttered the Vicar, stuffing the yellow handkerchief into his pocket. "Two murders within forty-eight hours! That Mr. Page had enemies I can understand, however deplorable that may be to contemplate. But Lady Codrington! She was a little—ah—careless in certain things, if you will, but in no manner a lady to inspire hatred or revenge. Who is this foul murderer? Who is he? Is he someone whom we know in the common round of our days? That is the terrifying thought I cannot escape."

Thus even the Vicar, who could scarcely be termed astute, had come to the conclusion that the murderer must be someone who had a part in the life of our small society. A stranger in Eastblyth never passed unnoticed, and everybody realised that. And for months no stranger had penetrated our parochial isolation.

I was wondering whether anybody in the library besides myself had observed the Vicar's barrenness of information concerning Lady Codrington's movements just before her death when the Inspector suddenly captured his attention by looking him closely in the eyes—somewhat melodramatically, I thought—and asked in a sharp, emphatic tone:

"Mr. Lake. *At what hour, this morning, did you meet Lady Codrington at Brooker's Mill?*"

The Vicar's round, pink jaw dropped, and a fish-like expression came upon his bucolic countenance.

"*I*—meet—Lady Codrington? I—I'm afraid you are mistaken, sir."

The Inspector pursed his lips, and regarded the clergyman as he would the boy he had caught throwing stones at a telegraph pole. The Vicar, one gathered from the Inspector's air, was telling an untruth. He was hiding a guilty secret, and he must reveal it.

"Come, come, Mr. Lake. Think again——"

Without waiting, however, for the Vicar to think again, he took from his pocket-case the letter Jupp had found in the dead woman's waste-paper basket, and with a gesture which reminded me of the way he had confronted Anita with the threatening letter she had written to Page, he thrust it in front of the Vicar's eyes.

"Is that your notepaper?"

"Y-yes," said the Vicar, blinking at it.

"And you wrote that letter, Mr. Lake! It is in your handwriting, and it is signed 'Lionel,' which is your name. It will save a lot of trouble if you will admit it——"

"And cause some," murmured Jupp, but I do not think the Inspector heard him. I am sure he was not meant to.

"But—but—that is, I shall have to read it before I can identify it," said the Reverend Lionel unhappily, and fumbled for his spectacles. The Inspector eyed him with an expression which said plainly: "All this beating about the bush won't help you," and waited while the agitated man put on his glasses and perused the letter.

He read it twice, turned it over doubtfully, glared at it, and finally snorted angrily.

"Forgery!" he said. "That is *not* my handwriting!" And he said it with much greater conviction than he could have achieved had he been speaking anything but the truth. He could not have learned to act that righteous indignation with a thousand years of practice.

"Not your handwriting?" repeated the Inspector, and glared interrogatively in my direction.

"At the time," I hastened to explain, "I said it 'appeared' to be the Vicar's handwriting. I am not an expert, but I certainly thought, and still think, that it is very like his handwriting."

"It is distinctly similar," admitted the Reverend Lionel. "Distinctly. I can understand Arden assuming that I had written it, although——"

"Can you understand Lady Codrington assuming that you had?"

The Vicar's face changed; he looked startled, and he coughed. Then horror came upon him, and he forgot to be pompous.

"She—*this* was used to lure her to her death?" he asked.

The Inspector, watching him narrowly, was convinced.

"Yes," he said. "We have every reason to believe that."

"Oh!" muttered the Vicar. "Oh! oh——!" And he sought a chair. The Inspector retrieved the forged letter and put it back in his pocket-case.

"I swear I didn't write it! I swear it!" cried the Reverend Lionel.

"All right. I'm prepared to imagine that some one obtained a sheet of the Vicarage note-paper and imitated your handwriting. It arrived at Lady Codrington's after dark last night——"

"Who delivered it?" asked the Vicar quickly.

"I wish I knew, or could find out. It was found by the servant in the letter-box."

"Ah! That is not the way *I* send a note. I always give it to one of my maids, who has instructions to ring the bell of the house to which it is addressed and hand it to whosoever opens the door, with the information either that there is 'no answer' or that she will wait for one. It is palpably absurd to suggest that *I* should creep up to 'Four Ways' and surreptitiously slip a letter in the box. Ridiculous!"

"Quite," agreed the Inspector. "Tell me, Mr. Lake; you see no reason why Lady Codrington should suspect that letter of being a forgery?"

The Vicar shrugged his fat shoulders.

"The writing is similar to mine, as I have said. Arden thought it was mine."

"Exactly. Then there is nothing out of the way in the contents which might have caused her to doubt that it was from you."

"Urh-um," said the Vicar, sitting suddenly upright. "I—that is—I cannot conceive myself arranging to meet any lady at such an hour at such a fantastic spot. It is five miles from the Vicarage and two from 'Four Ways.' In fact a—ah—a rendezvous of that kind suggests—er—an intimacy of friendship which I can assure you has never existed between us. Certainly not!"

I knew he was fibbing now, and both Jupp and the Inspector suspected it. The Vicar, however deep his hypocrisy, was a shocking bad liar. He puffed out his chest like a pigeon and blew his cheeks full of air, and repeated the words "Certainly not" with unnecessary vehemence. When I say I *knew* he was fibbing, I had heard the gossip which had insistently linked their names for the last three months. I have lived long enough in Eastblyth to discount by ninety-five per cent the stories the old ladies gestate and nourish over their tea-tables, but knowing the Vicar and knowing Lady Codrington, however, I had never seriously doubted but that a germ of truth lay somewhere in the birth of that particular story. Lady Codrington had always believed herself to be one of the most attractive and romantic women in the county, and it was more than likely that the Vicar's tenderness of heart where women were concerned had found him out when he came drifting within sound of her siren's song.

In short, the letter which had been used to get Lady Codrington out of bed to tramp two miles across the heath to an unfrequented spot on it could not have been better chosen—or rather forged. She had not paused an instant to question its authenticity, and if she had, its romantic glamour would have shouted down the feeble voice of caution.

"Clever," commented Jupp, and I realised that his alert mind, lacking though it did my knowledge of local gossip, had arrived at the only possible conclusion. He saw that Lady Codrington could no more have ignored the bait her murderer had prepared than escaped the fatal bullet with which he had awaited her.

The Inspector, on his part, probably decided that even if the Vicar had enjoyed a surreptitious affair with the dead woman (which would account for this distress of his on hearing of her murder) it was of no great importance save that she had been killed by someone who knew of it and had used it in setting his trap. It was quite obvious, at all events, that the Vicar had not been responsible for that particular letter, however many similar ones he may have written to the lady. The Inspector quite naturally and rightly returned to a practical point.

"Where do you keep your notepaper? In how many rooms at the Vicarage?" he asked.

"In my study, over the desk in a stationery rack."

"And the supply from which you fill the rack?"

"The top right-hand drawer of the desk."

"Nowhere else? Is that the only place in the house?"

"Yes."

"Good. We're getting on. It would be possible for someone to take a sheet of paper from that rack, and not be detected? Right. Now does it ever happen that persons other than the members of your household are admitted to your study and left there alone?"

The Vicar considered the question.

"It happens sometimes, certainly," he answered at length. "For instance, if I am out, but expected back soon, and someone calls on church or parish business, he or she is shown into the drawing-room or the study—the study if it is a man, the drawing-room if it is a lady. That is more or less the rule."

"I see. Let us assume, then, that there is someone who wants a piece of your notepaper. He could contrive to call on you with some adequate excuse, and time his arrival at a moment when he knew you would soon be returning home."

"You mean there was—that this cold-blooded, deliberate——"

"I want you please, Mr. Lake, to write me out a list of the people who have called on you on any business or pretext whatever during the last month, making a mark against the names of those whom you found awaiting you when you got home. It doesn't matter what time of the day or night it was, and I suggest that you use this calendar here to help you. Approximate dates would be valuable, if you could manage them. Thank you."

He shepherded the Vicar into the chair at the desk, put a pencil in his hand, and found him a piece of paper.

"Men and women, old and young, day and night—and mark the ones who arrived when you were out."

"I'll try," said the Vicar, like a dutiful child.

It was amazing to see the difference in the man. He had been thoroughly shaken, and although one could not hope that the pomposity had been for ever driven out of him, it was at least restful to see him without it.

The Inspector left the room to deal with the details of his administration, Jupp strolled out into the gathering twilight to survey the windows of Hamish Page's bedroom from the place it was presumed his slayer had fired the shot, Snarlett went over to examine the papers his clerk had unearthed, and I sat down to watch the Vicar at his compilation. He frowned over it, and bit the pencil, every now and again writing down a name as he remembered it.

For a space of some fifteen minutes the Eastblyth murder case seemed to enjoy a breathing space. Then, at the end of that time, the Inspector returned to imbue the library with his briskness. The Vicar looked up, and asked him a question.

"In the event of a person calling more than once during the month, Inspector, shall I make a note of it against his name? I mean there's the Professor's secretary, for instance

—young Blake. He called twice last week—the first time I was in, and the second time I fancy I was over in the vestry, and he was waiting when I——"

"Make a note of it! Make a note of it!" said the Inspector warmly, and he looked round for Jupp.

I was reminded of a terrier looking for a bone.

CHAPTER VII

Jupp reappeared a moment later, and the Inspector handed him the list. If the Vicar had not been present at the moment, I think English would have explained triumphantly that James Blake had called twice at the Vicarage during the week preceding the murders.

Jupp glanced through it.

"Nearly everybody in the neighbourhood," he said.

"Is my name there?" I asked, "because I rather think I looked in to see the Vicar either on the Friday or Saturday. He was at home, and we talked in the study."

"Your name is. Was that the same day Professor Skinner called?" asked Jupp. "His name appears next to yours."

"Yes, indeed I'm sure it was," interposed the Reverend Lionel. "Did I put a tick against him? He came about nine in the morning; indeed before I was dressed. He was in the study when I came down to breakfast. I remember he was smoking one of those strong cigars of his, and I told the maid to open both the windows when he had gone. I find the smell of cigar smoke gives me a most unpleasant nausea. He only stayed a moment or so."

"What did he want to see you about?" asked Jupp casually.

"Arden's scheme for the slum children. He came to protest against the camp being put on the foreshore. He said it spoilt the view from his bedroom and interfered with what he called his 'mental processes.' It seems he does most of his thinking in bed."

"The Professor is a terrible old lady in some ways," I said.

"Why did he go to the Vicar about the camp if Mr. Arden was responsible for it?" continued Jupp, in spite of the Inspector's air of wanting to remark that all this was quite irrelevant.

"The foreshore and marsh are mostly glebe land, and therefore under my jurisdiction," said the Vicar. "Arden thought it would be better for the boys if they were near the sea, and I agreed with him. The camp broke up two days ago, and, as I explained to the Professor, it was a very good cause, and in any case the tents would be gone in a week's time. He was very irritable, I thought, and quite unreasonable. He said he had no objection to Arden 'getting sociological' and trying to improve the health of the race, but surely the air on the heath, for instance, was quite as good as that by the sea. It was the same air, in fact, being scarcely a mile away. I explained the belief Arden had in sea and sun-bathing and all the rest of the advantages of the foreshore, but he could only think of the view from his bedroom windows."

"Very unreasonable of him," agreed Jupp. "And so he was alone with the paper rack?"

"No more alone with it than were the other six people on this list," said the Inspector, and read out a string of names: 'Mrs. Redcliffe, George Tupper, the Goodwins, Mr. Arden, Mr. Blake.' By the way, who are the Goodwins?"

"The Saxmundham Goodwins. They called to see my new herbaceous border. Brother and sister—charming people," replied the Vicar.

"I know them well—a very good family," Mr. Snarlett endorsed.

"Mrs. Redcliffe is the senior Mrs. Redcliffe?" continued the Inspector.

"Yes. She is a frequent caller—one of the Parish Trustees."

"Tell me, Arden," said Jupp, who seemed to be in a singularly tenacious mood. "Did Professor Skinner come to you about this spoilt view after he had failed to move the Vicar?"

71

"No. I expect he decided to put up with it for another week."

"It sounds ridiculous, not to say inhuman, to make a fuss about what was, after all, a charitable action. I assume it was charitable?"

"Entirely. I pay the expenses of the camp every year out of my own pocket. Skinner probably realised he would get no sympathy from me. He *is* inhuman. It may be his scientific mind. Although I'm damned if I see how a man with a fine brain can devote it to the development of purely destructive principles the way he does without stamping his conscience underfoot!"

I suppose I spoke with greater feeling than was really necessary under the circumstances, for I was aware that they were all looking at me.

"True, true," murmured the Vicar, who was recovering his poise. "A deplorable thing——".

"You take these things seriously, Mr. Arden," observed Jupp.

"Arden is one of the few people I know who practises what he preaches," said the Vicar with a sigh. I realised what the sigh meant. He was thinking about his chancel, and wondering whether he dare approach me for a subscription, well knowing that I was somewhat critical of his church, although a lover of ancient buildings.

"I don't know what hare you are chasing," the Inspector remarked to Jupp, "but to my mind it is clear that Professor Skinner is just the sort of man to be annoyed by a spoilt view to the extent of complaining about it to the man he deemed responsible."

"When are we going to visit the Professor?" asked Jupp.

"——and his secretary. As soon as you like," the Inspector replied briskly.

"Why not now?"

"Certainly."

"The car is outside," I said, for I wanted to be present at what looked like being one of the most important moments in the Inspector's case. He glanced at me with a smile.

"I am very glad to have you with me, Mr. Arden, on these occasions. Quite often you produce a useful piece of information at the right time. If I may say so, you have the makings of a deductive mind."

"And Jupp has already detected a psychological aspect in it. I shall be a complete detective before I know what's happened to me."

Before the Vicar departed, the Inspector asked him for what purpose James Blake had called on those two occasions, and learnt that it had been to borrow volumes one and two of Gibbon's *Decline and Fall of the Roman Empire*.

"Mr. Blake," the Vicar explained, "is a serious student of history in his spare time, which, if not plentiful, is surely fruitful. One could wish that all young men nowadays employed their leisure as sensibly."

"Yes, yes," agreed English, and having warned him that he might be required at the inquests, ushered him shuddering out of the library.

We set off on the short drive to "Windy Arbour," where the Skinners, father and daughter, had lived for the last eight years. It was a modern two-storey house of white stucco, but not unpleasant design. Outbuildings, a garage, and two big barn-like erections which were workshops, occupied the rear of the house. By reason of the slight rise on which it was built and the absence of any trees immediately in front of it, the eastern aspect enjoyed a wide panorama of sea and gently curving coast-line. Behind it were oak and pine woods through which a private road led from the main Eastblyth-Inderswick route.

"Admirable spot to work in peace," was Jupp's verdict when we came in sight of it.

The sound of the car brought a man into the drive two hundred yards from the house. The Inspector asked me to stop for a moment, and he got out to talk to him. I realised he was a plain-clothes detective, who had been detailed to watch the house, and it showed me how careful English was being. Jupp eyed the conference gloomily, and said something about the efficiency of the police force and how it was driving hard-working criminals out of business. "Tell me about the Professor," he said. "I want another of your word-portraits."

"A tall, thin, bald, energetic man, a really first-class mathematician with a practical, inventive brain. Undoubtedly a great armament expert—he has the War Office and the Admiralty in his pocket. He is independent in thought and action, impatient of anything which smacks of stupidity, and is quite lacking in the paternal instinct—vide Anita—who is afraid of him. He lives for his work, and spends sixteen hours out of the twenty-four with it."

"Money?"

"Small private income, and a continual stream of grants from the Government. At least, until recently there has been. This general disarmament fever—I daren't hope it is anything more—has had an effect on it. I don't believe there is the money there was for his activities. One or two things he has said lately suggest it. There's this long-ranged field gun of his—I know he is finding the experimental stage more costly than he expected. He told me so the other day."

"I see. What is his age?"

"Sixty; but looks fifty or less. Well preserved, and unusually vigorous."

"Has Blake been with him long?"

"Five years."

"They get along well together?"

"Excellently I believe. Blake is bright—a Senior Wrangler——"

"Armament expert too?"

"Yes, but his interests are more general. For instance, he invented a gas mask which put the Professor in a rage for weeks because it quite obviated the lethal qualities of a new poison gas the Professor had achieved."

"A chemist also, the Professor?"

"Yes. He has an amazing scientific scope."

At this moment the Inspector returned to the car, the plain-clothes man stepped off the road into the trees, and we drove on toward the house.

"The girl appears to have come straight home after she left us," English said. "Blake is in the workshop nearest the house with Professor Skinner. We'll go up to the front door, and I shall ask to see the Professor."

"Have you met him before?" asked Jupp.

"No."

The reason for Jupp's question became apparent within half a minute of the Inspector pressing the bell. The door was opened by Carstairs, the butler. Before the Inspector had handed him his card, or indeed said a word, Carstairs addressed himself to me.

"The Professor asks you to step this way, if you please, sir, while the Inspector and the other gentleman wait in the lounge."

The Inspector frowned. In the first place he had not expected the Professor to know that he was going to call on him, and in the second he did not understand why I should be singled out for an interview. He was not sure whether to feel slighted or not.

"The Professor," vouchsafed Carstairs confidentially to me, "is in one of his moods."

"I think I had better go to him," I said.

"All right," said the Inspector, "and I would be very glad if you would explain to him that it is of the utmost importance that I should see him as soon as possible."

Jupp said nothing, but he seemed a trifle less gloomy than usual.

So I left them in the lounge, and went out with Carstairs through the side door across the courtyard into the first workshop, wondering with some interest which particular mood of the great man's I was to find him in. It was six o'clock, and according to unchanging habit, the Professor, Anita and James Blake should have been in the lounge when we arrived, drinking sherry or whisky-and-soda.

Instead, all three of them were in the workshop, and my first impression of them amongst the lathes and leather driving-belts, the glimmer of blue steel and the chaos of tools

75

and appliances, was that each was in the grip of nervous tension. The Professor was thunderous, Anita pale and thoughtful as though she had just emerged from some mental ordeal, and James Blake darkly and morosely defiant. His rather heavy jaw was thrust forward, his straight, thick black eyebrows were drawn together, and he sat on the edge of a bench in his blue overalls with his hands thrust deep into his pockets, his wiry black hair more on end than usual. He favoured me with a quick, anxious glance as I entered, Anita did not look at me, and the Professor began talking in a growling monotone the moment he had shaken hands with me.

"Blake saw your car from the window up there," he jerked his head in the direction of the ladder which led up to the rooms above the workshop. "Anita tells me you are muddled up in this police investigation. Is that correct?"

"Muddled up?" I said cautiously. "I have seen something of it, and driven Inspector English about the countryside to-day, viewing bodies and questioning people. It's all very interesting to watch. Also there's a man called Jupp staying with me at the Manor whom Page commissioned to look into the situation before he was killed."

"*George* Jupp?"

"Yes."

The Professor nodded and said:

"A singularly able gentleman. Scotland Yard has been trying to attach him to it for months. I haven't met him, but I've heard of him. Well, Arden, Anita has apparently been doing her best to make a mess of things, one way and another. She came home to tea, to Blake here, with a story about this Inspector fellow thinking Blake shot Page and Lady Codrington. She didn't tell me—she never tells me anything—but Blake, who is quite intelligent, realised that I ought to know all about it. He insisted that I should be told. They've just told me. I haven't had time to go into the details of the business, but I don't think I need to. I can see that this Inspector of yours is barking up the wrong tree, and——"

"He isn't mine, and Anita *has* been foolish."

"Rub it in," said Anita.

"Be quiet, can't you!" snapped her father. "I'm talking." Anita subsided.

"I gather," he continued, "that he has turned up here to pursue his inquiries, making Blake his particular object. He thinks Blake and Anita between them slaughtered Page to stop his blackmailing and get his money, and presumably Lady Codrington because she had stumbled on something which gave them away. Well, it's ridiculous nonsense, and I'm not going to stand for it! Blake, did you kill Page?"

"No, but I should have liked to——"

"What you would have liked to do has got nothing to do with what you didn't do. You didn't kill Page?"

"I did not."

"Nor the Codrington woman?"

"Nor Lady Codrington."

"That's good enough for me," said the Professor. "And Anita had no more to do with it than Blake had. She swears she hadn't. Swear it, Anita."

"I swear it."

It was not until afterwards, when I came to look back on the conversation, that I realised how fantastic it was. The casual way the Professor asked them if they had committed the murder or not was as unreal as anything could have been.

"There you are!" he cried at me. "Now you go, like a good chap, and tell this Inspector what you've just heard. I'm very busy, and I can't spare Blake for any nonsensical inquiry. He doesn't know a damned thing which could be the slightest bit of use to the police; and if that Inspector starts pushing his nose in here I shall be very angry. Very angry indeed!"

He was already simmering with rage which would require but small encouragement to burst forth into some violent action; never had I seen him so stirred, and I realised what an autocrat the man was. He ruled his house and the lives of the two people with whom he was in daily contact with an unquestioned dominance. If Anita succeeded in living wildly, even loosely, it was behind his back; if James Blake cherished a passion for her, it was secretly and without her father's knowledge. Such matters would have interfered with his sacred routine, and his impatience with those responsible would have been catastrophic. I was not surprised to observe that while he had lost some of his anxiety now that he had demonstrated the innocence of his daughter and his assistant, they, on the other hand, showed no relief. They knew as well as I did that the Inspector was not at all likely to be put off by the message intimating that he must look elsewhere for the murderer. They knew that before they came to the end of the affair they would first see the Professor considerably more angry than he was now, and the prospect weighed upon them. I would have liked Jupp to be present in the workshop at that moment; his impressions would have been interesting. He would have realised, I think, that English was right in saying Blake was in love with Anita..

"You tell the Inspector," repeated the Professor, and waited expectantly for me to leave the workshop. But I hesitated.

"Well?" he said.

"Inspector English," I explained, "is rather a persistent, careful kind of man. I think he will want to ask a few questions."

"I haven't the time, and I haven't the inclination to answer them! Or to permit anyone else to! Blake has the new alloy in that furnace over there, and he has got to keep a constant eye on it. Anita, I understand, has already answered too many questions. You aren't trying to tell me you don't believe them when they say they had nothing to do with the murders?"

"I am perfectly sure they hadn't—but then I'm not a police inspector. Police inspectors seem to arrive at their conclusions in a roundabout way. However, I'll tell him what you want me to tell him, but I doubt if it will have much effect."

I went back to the lounge, where Jupp and the Inspector were sitting opposite one another. Jupp had his eyes closed, and his head rested on a cushion.

"He says he feels tired," remarked the Inspector. "Well, where's the Professor? I must——"

"The Professor," I said, "asked me to tell you that neither his daughter nor Blake committed the murders. And he's too busy, and cannot be disturbed."

He rose to his feet, stared at me.

"Oh?" he said. "So neither of them committed the murders? How did he discover that?"

"He asked them if they did, and they said no."

"Good Lord! What else did he expect them to say? What arrant nonsense! And he's very busy, and cannot be disturbed, is he? Does he realise what we're up against—that two dastardly murders have been done in the midst of a peaceful village, and that the person who did them has *got* to be discovered? I thought the man had a brain!"

"He has, and it seems to be occupied with a new alloy."

"Stuff!" cried the Inspector, and put his finger on the bell-push by the fireplace. He kept it there until Carstairs appeared.

"Sir?"

The Inspector removed his finger from the bell.

"Kindly take this card to Professor Skinner, and tell him I would be very much obliged if he would grant me a few moments of his valuable time. I wish to see him on a matter of extreme urgency and importance. I am here in an official capacity."

Carstairs took the card, bowed slightly, and left the room.

Jupp awoke.

"When a man like Professor Skinner says definitely that somebody hasn't committed a murder, he's more likely to be right than wrong."

The Inspector bridled.

"When a man like Professor Skinner comes to a decision concerning something outside his particular sphere of knowledge and experience, he cannot be regarded in it as an expert. Professor Skinner is a specialist in one direction; I am a specialist in another. This matter happens to be in my department, not in his."

Jupp lifted a languid hand, and pointed at the bookshelf above the Inspector's head.

"I wonder whether that's a ·35 or a ·22?" he asked meditatively, and the Inspector swung round.

"On top of the Shakespeare," added Jupp, whose sharp eyes had caught the dull shine of a rifle barrel in the space between the books and the shelf above. The Inspector reached up, and gingerly lifted down the weapon.

"No dust on it," he remarked, and added quickly: "It's a ·22 all right!"

He handled it very carefully, presumably lest he should smear any finger-prints there might be on it, and an expression of intent satisfaction came into his face.

"This could have fired those bullets!" he said. "At least, it could have fired the one that killed Hamish Page. We haven't actually extracted Lady Codrington's, but judging by the size of the wound in the forehead, this might——"

"Found the weapon, have you?" said the Professor from the door, and he slammed it behind him in a fruitless effort to relieve his feelings. He glared at the policeman. "Well, sir, and what can I do for you?"

I was sorry for English, who after all was merely doing his difficult duty. It gave him no pleasure to have aroused the Professor's wrath; indeed, he must have deplored it, since it would certainly make the man an unsatisfactory source of information. As it was, I think he handled the situation very well.

"I assure you, Professor," he said, "I would not trouble you, take you from your work, if this business was not a terribly serious one in which we cannot afford to ignore the slightest clue, the smallest sign, that looks as though it might lead us in the right direction. There are certain questions I shall have to ask you, either now or in the witness-box. The choice is yours, sir, and if I might suggest it, your having to appear at an inquest, and perhaps at a trial held at the Assize Court many miles away, would more seriously interrupt your work than to answer me the few questions I propose to put to you now."

"Huh!" said the Professor through his nose, and sat himself

down in a chair facing the Inspector, who placed the small rifle on the table and at once began his questions.

They dealt solely with James Blake: the length of time he had been with the Professor, the kind of life he led when he was not in the workshop, and a variety of other aspects of the young man. The Professor answered them shortly, and occasionally with impatience, as though he could see no point in them. James Blake was keen on his work, brilliant occasionally, spent all his spare time reading history and science, slept over the workshop partly because it was his choice, partly to guard the precious secrets which from time to time it sheltered. He rarely left the estate, except in winter for a little duck-shooting up the Blyth estuary.

So he shot duck? The Inspector was interested. Had he made any spectacular bags?

Once or twice he had brought home as many as twenty brace after three hours in a duck-punt in the early morning. Yes, he was probably a good shot.

"Whose is that rifle?" asked the Inspector suddenly, indicating the .22.

"Mine," said the Professor tersely.

"Who uses it?"

"I really haven't an idea. I know that I don't."

"There isn't a speck of dust on it," observed the Inspector.

"The maids do their work, I suppose."

Jupp strolled over to the table, and bent down to scrutinise the end of the barrel. He returned to his seat without saying anything.

"No sign of a silencer having been used on it?" asked the Professor, and the Inspector, startled, also examined it.

"Not a sign," agreed Jupp. "It certainly isn't threaded for the screw-on type, and there isn't the faintest indication that it has had the other kind on it—the push-on sort."

"How did you know, Professor Skinner, that we had decided the murderer used a silenced rifle?" asked the Inspector.

"I was having dinner with Mr. Arden the night someone shot at him from the wood," he retorted. "There were six of us at the table, and none of us heard a report—only the smack of the bullet against the panelling. That was earlier the same night on which Page was killed. I gather that since he was not found until the morning, and had been dead some hours, there was no report to hear on that occasion also." He spoke as one would explain a simple point to a dense child, but the Inspector refused to be ruffled.

"However," added the Professor, "I expect there are some more ·22's about somewhere—we may as well have them out and look at them." He rang the bell. Of Carstairs he requested:

"Ask Mr. Blake to bring all the ·22 rifles he can find—to bring them to me here."

The Inspector was neither sure that he wanted to see James Blake at the moment, nor sure that it was a good idea to have him look for the ·22 rifles. In a way the message Carstairs was taking was a warning one; it showed the trend of the investigation. But one could do nothing about it. In any case it was unlikely that Blake would bring the particular rifle with which he had killed the millionaire and Lady Codrington.

In a very short time Blake came in with three ·22 rifles of different makes. The Inspector devoured his face, and perhaps realised the mental power and tenacity of purpose of the young man with whom he had got to deal. Blake put the rifles on the table with a clatter, and noticing the one which we had found on the bookshelf, remarked:

"Oh, you've got the other Remington here. I thought it was in the store-room in No. 2." Then, deliberately, I believe, he added a thoroughly damaging statement. Perhaps he was still in a defiant mood, perhaps he knew that the Inspector would get the information elsewhere in any case. At all events, he said casually:

"I expect I forgot to put it back on Thursday—or was it Wednesday, Professor? It was the day last week you had to go to Bungay to see Sir John Matthews."

The Inspector snapped at the morsel like a hungry dog. As the Professor said "Thursday" he asked quickly:

"You took this rifle from the store-room in No. 2 last Thursday? What did you do with it?"

Blake raised his black eyebrows.

"I used up a couple of hundred cartridges on the beach. Target-shooting, you know. Keeps the eye in. The duck season will be starting in a month or so."

"What target did you use?"

"Moving ones. I chuck old tins into the sea—you find them along the high-tide mark—and sink 'em. A couple of shots; these ·22's are very accurate. Mr. Arden taught me the tin trick. He used to do it too, a couple of years ago."

"I remember," I said, "but I used a slightly bigger bore, I think."

The Inspector looked at me reproachfully, as though he thought I might have told him before about Blake's target-shooting on the beach.

"Do you often 'keep your eye in' like that, Mr. Blake?"

"Oh, now and again. One doesn't get much opportunity, though. We work pretty hard here."

The Inspector nodded, and gazed reflectively at the collection of rifles. Any one of them might be the weapon with which the murders had been committed.

"I will take those away with me," he said, and turned to Blake. There was nothing in his expression to warn the young man of the very significant question which he now flung at him.

"Can you account for your movements during a period commencing at nine-thirty on the night of the tenth until seven o'clock the following morning?"

Whatever James Blake may have felt at that moment, he betrayed no emotion.

"In other words," he said evenly, "what was I doing the night Hamish Page was murdered. I'll tell you, Inspector. The Professor and Miss Skinner were dining at the Manor; I went to bed early, somewhere between nine and ten, read Gibbon's *Decline and Fall* until half-past eleven, turned out the light, and went immediately to sleep. At eight-thirty, I awoke, put on a dressing-gown, walked across the courtyard to my bath, and was seen on my way to it by Anne Fisher, one of the house-maids. Between nine o'clock in the evening, when I said good-night to Carstairs after dinner and went to my room over the workshop—I am quite alone in the building at night—and the moment Anne passed me in the corridor, I saw nobody and was seen by nobody. In fact I haven't the ghost of an alibi."

"It doesn't look as if you had," agreed the Inspector, who I think found himself better impressed by James Blake than he had expected to be. "It seems too," he added, "from the conciseness of your account of that night, that you anticipated questions concerning it?"

"That is perfectly true," said Blake. "From what Miss Skinner told me of her afternoon with you I realised the direction of your suspicion. But I would like to state, before this proceeds further, that I did not kill Hamish Page."

The Inspector nodded.

"I am going to ask you to make a statement to-morrow morning, and for that purpose it would be convenient if you would call at the police-station. About half-past eleven would——"

"Confound it!" the Professor burst out. "This is exactly what I expected. James, if you've any sense at all, you'll refuse to make any statements. I'm going to wire to my solicitors for Critchley-Jenkins. He'll know what to do! This damned inquiry has got to be stopped! I won't have it! It's no use talking to me, Inspector; no use at all. Arden, tell him it's no use! I've got work to do, and he must be made to realise it! Blake's time belongs to me, and I need it—every minute of it!"

He stamped out of the room, and his protesting voice died away as he crossed the courtyard to his beloved workshop. The Inspector appeared to be unmoved.

"How many cartridges have you left?" he asked Blake, who had remained standing by the table.

"Three hundred and fifty—four hundred. Thereabouts."

"I will take them with the rifles, please."

Blake walked across to a cabinet in the corner by the window, and returned with eight small cardboard boxes, which he placed on the table.

"Seven full ones, and a few left in the eighth," he remarked. "I see the necessity of this inquiry, Inspector, and I will do my best to get over to the police-station to-morrow morning."

"Thank you. And just one more thing while we're dealing with this business of the rifles. The Professor has a Fire-arms Certificate, of course. Are all the weapons in his possession entered on it, do you know?"

"They are. It's part of my work to see that it is kept up to date. Firearm manufacturers send us stuff every so often, and it has to be registered with the East Suffolk Police. If you'd like to take the certificate, I'll get it for you."

"I'd be much obliged. I want to check these ·22's."

While the young man was gone, the Inspector shook his head.

"He's being too helpful. In my experience, an innocent man in his position is either frightened or angry, and he appears to be neither."

"Mm," said Jupp, which might have been agreement or difference.

Then Blake returned with the Firearm's Certificate, which the Inspector slipped into his pocket. We prepared to depart with the armoury which had been collected. I noticed that Blake's dark eyes flickered restlessly. He was showing nervousness at last, but not on his own account. He could not forget that Anita was embroiled in this dangerous business.

Sudden pity for him came over me. He had spent too much of his life at bench and drawing-board to have learnt anything about women. He worshipped the ground beneath Anita's feet, and it occurred to me that he could have travelled the world over and failed to find a less worthy goddess. He was clever and he was honest, where she was merely sharp-witted and cunning. He would be clay in her sex-wise fingers.

He seemed very much alone, standing there while we filed out of the room, and I obeyed an impulse. I paused, and said quietly, so that the Inspector did not hear:

"Come over to dinner to-night, if you'd care to. About eight suit you?"

He gave me a doubtful glance, realised the friendliness of my motive, and at once accepted. We shook hands, and I followed the others to the car.

"What about a drink with us, Inspector?" I suggested as we set off. "I'll drive you over to Southwold afterwards."

"Thanks, Mr. Arden. I've had rather an afternoon of it, one way and another."

We reached the Manor about six-thirty, and I was greeted by Jeames with the news that there was a gentleman to see me in the drawing-room.

"He wouldn't give his name, sir, although I made sure he wasn't one of them reporters. He says he knows you well, sir —and in fact that he knows me also, although I must say I don't think I've ever set eyes on him before."

I exchanged glances with Jupp and the Inspector.

"I'll bet he *is* a reporter, though," said English.

I took the ·45 from my hip-pocket, and slipped it into my right-hand jacket pocket. I kept my hand on it.

"Let's take a look at him, anyway," I said.

The three of us, with Jeames close at our heels, went down the hall to the drawing-room. I opened the door. The man who was sitting in an arm-chair jumped to his feet, and advanced with a smile which wrinkled his eyes. He was the red-bearded man I had seen outside The Knife and Whistle.

Then, in a flash of memory, I saw him without the beard.

"Good evening, Mr. Mendholz," I said.

The Inspector stiffened, Jupp coughed, and Mr. Mendholz laughed. He extended his hand.

"Ah!" he cried. "But vat a joke! I thought, vill mine old enemy remember me—vill he? Or shall I hav to remind him of me—whom he saw but vonce?"

He laughed again, genially, and grasped my hand, which I took out of my pocket.

"Zo!" he said. "You carry a pistol, hein?" His eyes were sharp.

"I'm sorry," I apologised. "But we've had a murder or so in the neighbourhood."

"Ah, yes. The village is in great eggsitement. I came from Norwich this morning. I sell pianos for Brodekheimer. I sell them to your English provinces. Ah, but it is difficult. Your provinces are not musical, nein. I see your name in the telephone-book. I come in my leedle motor-car, to shake the hand of mine old enemy. Ah—those were zee days, *nicht war*?"

Was the man a greater actor than I had ever suspected? Or was this a genuine burying of the hatchet? For the life of me I could not tell at that moment. My mind was perhaps already so full of stuff. The Inspector broke in with a gruff question.

"Norwich last night, Mr. Mendholz?"

"Yes. And Ipswich to-morrow—no, indeed to-night. I hav a room booked at The White Hart. *Ya, mien frendt.* You do not believe?"

The Inspector did not reply, but asked another question.

"And at Norwich. You were there how long, and where did you stay?"

"The King's Arms, for four nights."

I was sorry for Mendholz for the first time since I had known him. This seemed a poor greeting for a man who had come to make peace.

"In the meantime," murmured Jupp unexpectedly, "what about that drink?"

It relieved the situation. We sought the tantulus in the library, and over it reviewed the position. Mendholz, however dulled by piano-selling, realised that for some reason perhaps not unconnected with the past he was under suspicion. The Inspector eyed him narrowly, and I saw that he was itching to be at the telephone and talking to The King's Arms. Jupp drank sherry with the air of a man who is enjoying a moment's leisure.

"I think, Mr. Mendholz," said the Inspector finally, "that it might be advisable for you to stay here, or in Southwold, for to-night."

Mendholz bowed. Perhaps, like all Germans, he respected and feared the police; perhaps he wisely recognised the inevitable. If Inspector English suspected a man, he suspected him. Mendholz wanted to sell pianos in England; it would not be sensible to antagonise anybody in authority. Who knows what he thought? I certainly hadn't an idea.

"I will take a room at the inn in the village where I had lunch," said Mendholz, and raised his glass to me.

The Inspector accompanied him to the gate, and I expect he detailed the constable there to see that the German did not stray from The Knife and Whistle.

"Well?" said Jupp when they had gone.

I shrugged my shoulders.

I had never approved of Mendholz, and I did not suppose that I ever would.

CHAPTER VIII

As far as the investigation was concerned, nothing further was attempted by the Inspector that day save to communicate with Norwich. I drove him to Southwold, where we left him. His mood was one of exasperation. Mendholz had complicated things. But for him, Blake looked like the answer. A few details here and there, a little more evidence of Blake's infatuation for Anita, evidence of his prowess with a .22 rifle, a search for the silencer—he had few hopes, however, of getting hold of that—and the jury at some not very future sitting of the adjourned inquests would bring in a verdict against the two of them. To-morrow afternoon at Page's inquest he would produce evidence of identification, manner of death, and so on, and ask for a fortnight's adjournment. He would see the coroner in the morning, and explain the situation. A fortnight was plenty of time; mercifully everything was comfortably localised, and there would be necessity for very little outside inquiry. Blake's past would have to be looked into; one never knew but what there might not be something in it to indicate the potential murderer, although, of course, when passion played a part, it could turn the feet of the most respectable of men into lawless paths. English was sure, also, that the Skinner servants would have plenty to say about the emotional attachment of their mistress and her father's servants. Servants never missed that kind of thing. . . .

Thus we left him, and returned to the Manor about seven, stopping at The Knife and Whistle on the way to pick up Jupp's suitcase. The prospect of a quiet evening, Jupp explained, and an opportunity to talk freely after so many hours in contact with a mind already made up, which the Inspector's had been almost from the moment he had met him, was gratifying.

"James Blake," I said, "is coming to dinner, so you'll have to talk later, when he has gone."

"I shall talk now. So you asked him to dinner?"

"I may be able to help him, although things look black enough against him."

"They do."

"Half the village," I pointed out, "knows he is a crack shot with exactly that type of rifle, the girl he loves was being blackmailed into marriage by the man who has been murdered, and there isn't a night in the year for which he could produce a cast-iron alibi. Apart from the blackmail motive, if it doesn't seem strong enough, there is that of a vast fortune to be gained for the girl he wants to marry. Further, there are four rifles for him to choose from, and three hundred and fifty odd cartridges from which to select two—or rather four, counting the attempts."

"Thank you," said Jupp, "that's the Inspector's case simply and adequately stated. Now let us look at the defence. We mustn't consider the obvious thing which prevents a James Blake from using the method of killing he is well known to use on old tins he finds on the beach: his intelligence. If Page had died of a stomach ache, or fallen under a steam-roller, we might have suspected Mr. Blake, but he did neither. We will look only at the tangible evidence. One, the absence of any marks of a silencer on those four rifles. I looked at them carefully in the car just now. Two, Blake says he spent all that night in bed; prove he didn't. In other words, was he seen away from the house by anybody at any hour when he says he was in bed? So far, nobody has turned up to tell us that they saw him. They may yet, of course, but I can't help feeling that we should have heard about it by now if we were going to. As for the Codrington murder—which you did not mention—as far as I can see the only evidence against our young friend is the fact that he called on the Vicar twice, and on one occasion was left alone to steal from the notepaper rack. If he had been the only person to have had that chance during the last month it would be a more significant fact, but dozens of other people appear to have been in that study alone, or in the company of a short-sighted, unobservant clergyman who I don't suppose was keeping an especial eye on his note-paper. Admittedly it would be easier to lay hands on it when he was not in the room, but I'm almost certain I could find or make an opportunity to take a sheet when he was there. I'm afraid the notepaper stealing is a weak point in the Inspector's case. No jury in its senses would regard it as complete evidence; the Vicar's study is too much like a club waiting-room, and the defence would make a lot of that. You see how easy it is to argue down purely circumstantial evidence."

"And yet circumstantial evidence has hung men—and women."

"Certainly, although not many in recent years. In the nine-teenth century it was more successful. By 'women,' you were thinking of Miss Skinner?"

"I suppose so, yes."

"She's the chink in Blake's armour," said Jupp, "and the Inspector knows it. She completes the picture so admirably. If I'm not wrong, he proposes to put an ingenious alternative: Did she conspire with Blake that he should kill Page and, later, Lady Codrington, or did she merely discover afterwards that he was guilty, and strive, in various practical ways, to destroy dangerous evidence, such as her knowledge of Page's Will and the letter she had written him? Was she *pretending* to be upset when I blurted out the rumour I had heard? That's how the Inspector will present it, through the Public Prosecutor, and in the scurry of wondering exactly what happened between the couple the jury will be side-tracked from considering the possibility that they are both innocent."

We were silent for a moment.

"It all sounds very grim," I said finally. "And frankly I don't understand the Inspector's attitude. It has so little to do with justice."

"You mean he's determined to get a conviction, and ignores the fact that he may be entirely wrong? He does; but it's a subconscious process of mind. It's his job to find the murderer; if he doesn't, he gets into trouble with the Press, and perhaps with his superiors. Isn't it natural that he should look only as far as he can see?"

I led the way to the decanter again.

"It is easy for you and me to be critical of his methods," he went on, "and formulate theories of our own. The *need* to produce results is not upon us. This is one of the most remarkable sherries I have tasted in this country; if you will forgive me. . . ."

He allowed it to permeate the tip and sides of his tongue, aerated it, that the ethers might be released, by drawing in a short breath through slightly open lips, and allowed it to mount his palate—the expert tasting his wine.

Having savoured it to his satisfaction, he added:

"Did the Professor run true to form this evening?"

I considered the question for a moment, and he helped me out.

"Was he more unreasonable, shall we say, than usual?"

"That expresses it," I agreed. "He struck me as being rather more conscious of the gravity of the situation than he pretended, and I think it was on Anita's account. If you noticed, Blake occupied the stage, and Anita's name was scarcely mentioned."

"That happened, and it may have been intentional on the Professor's part, and it certainly was on Blake's. But the thing which struck me most was his definitely anti-social attitude. The fact that a murderer is at large, presumably in the district, does not matter a damn to him as long as his peace and privacy are not interfered with. By all means look for the criminal, but look for him elsewhere, sort of thing. It was queer, to tell you the truth, Arden; he behaved much more like a guilty man trying to follow some obscure method of conceal-ment than did young Blake. And that is my considered opinion.

"*The Professor!*" I exclaimed. "You think——"

"If I were to hear that Lady Codrington had set her romantic cap at the Professor, and had refused to take 'no' for an answer, or some such complication, I would be quite as willing to suppose he killed her to be rid of her as the Inspector is to believe that Blake killed her because she had some knowledge of the Page murder."

"But good Heavens, man! Who is his accomplice? Who shot at me during that dinner, when the Professor was with me in the room? Blake and Anita are natural accomplices together if you like, but Skinner is alone—unless Blake . . . but no; Blake is as much in the dark as anybody—he isn't implicated anywhere, I'm dead sure of it——"

"Just a minute. May I refill this glass? Thanks. Now listen. The Professor has invented quite a number of interesting pieces of ordnance, hasn't he? Can you remember any of them? Their types, names, purposes—anything about them?"

I stared at him. He jumped about so in this conversational mood. The Professor's inventions?

"Before I caught the train at Liverpool Street this morning," he went on, "I took the trouble to look up the local directory of this district to get some sort of an idea of the kind of place it was, and the type of people who lived in it. The Professor's name and yours were the two which stood out particularly. You were both known to the larger world, the Professor to the point of being an international figure. I looked him up in one or two reference books. It may sound an odd thing to do, but it was not due to any method of mine; it was simply that I felt uncertain what exactly he was famous for—what his chief occupation was. Well and good. Do you remember just before the war there was an uproar in the papers about a thing called 'The Silent Skinner'?"

I shook my head.

"I was big-game hunting all through the winter and spring of 1913 to 1914. I missed it, I expect, or else I've forgotten it. 'The Silent Skinner'?"

"A boy in Catford, or maybe it was Streatham, got into trouble with an old lady who kept cats—dozens of cats. It seems that the boy who lived next door, either took a dislike to the cats or else he had sporting instincts. At all events, it was observed that now and again a cat taking the air in the old lady's backyard would suddenly give a kind of jump and fall down dead. It was very mysterious, and remained so for several weeks, until it was discovered that they died quite ordinarily by the passage of a small bullet through some vital organ. The subsequent investigations brought to light a number of knot holes in the fence, and in the possession of the small boy a 'Silent Skinner,' then on the market at eighteen-and-six. It was a compact and practically noiseless air-pistol. The old lady was a little deaf, and she did not hear the soft 'phut' of the discharge through the knot-hole nearest the doomed cat. Her prosecution of the cat-killing small boy led to the uproar in the papers about the danger of allowing air-pistols, and in particular 'The Silent Skinner,' to come into the hands of the young. The excitement did not lead anywhere, except that 'The Silent Skinner' enjoyed quite a boom for a while, but it never caught on, chiefly I suspect because small boys prefer an air-pistol which not only makes a bit of an explosion when the trigger is pulled, but is also capable of a more practical range than a mere six yards—and that was the whole trouble with 'The Silent Skinner.' Its designer, in an effort to reduce the sound of its discharge, had reduced its range to comparatively negligible proportions. In fact 'The Silent Skinner,' although mentioned in the reference books as being of Professor Gilbert Skinner's invention, can never have been one of his brightest efforts. You see my point?"

"I'm afraid, Jupp, I don't. If you are showing me that the Professor may have committed the murders, I don't see how a 'Silent Skinner' can have helped him in them—with its range of six yards."

"One question, then. Was your dinner-party sitting in silence when that bullet smashed your wine-glass and hit the wall behind your head?"

"No. The Vicar, as far as I remember, was laughing at something Lady Codrington had just said."

Jupp held up his sherry to the evening glow, and peered into its pale yellow depths.

"I have met the Vicar twice," he said, "but neither occasion has been one on which his laughter would have been suitable, so I have not heard it. But I am almost certain that if it is at all a normal laugh it is quite loud enough to drown the soft 'phut' of a 'Silent Skinner' fired in the same room with it."

"Good God!" I said.

Jupp finished his sherry, and inquired gloomily:

"Where at the table in relation to you was the Professor sitting?"

"Opposite me."

He nodded.

"And he was the first to say that it was obviously a rifle bullet. Nobody questioned it. . . . The open window helped the illusion."

"He—he meant to kill me?" I said.

"Heavens, no! As I suggested as a theory some time this morning, and as the Inspector thinks even now, although he attributes it to someone else and to another weapon—that was an alibi-maker."

I rubbed my forehead.

"My head is beginning to go round—and it isn't the sherry. Jupp, what damned ingenuity!"

"Mine? Or the Professor's?"

"Both."

"If both can claim it."

"Eh?" I said.

"I mean, the Professor may not have thought of it."

I poured myself another sherry, and drank it while Jupp remarked:

"It's just another beautiful theory with a fact clinging to it here and there. I suppose," he added wistfully, "you don't know any secret history connecting Lady Codrington with our scientist?"

"I don't. But the Vicar would—if there is any."

"I shall ask him. In fact I think I will visit him after dinner to-night, while you are holding Blake's hand and telling him not to be alarmed."

"All right," I said. "There's one thing, though. Haven't you also failed to put up a motive for the Professor's killing of Page?"

"But that must be obvious!" he exclaimed. "Disarmament fever—all the nations cutting down armament expenditure, including ourselves. British Government falling short in its grants for the Professor's experiments. His work is his life, and he has got to the stage where he can't stop for a moment. Must go on. Must have money. *Money!* Hamish Page has told him that he has made a Will in Anita's favour. Page is too healthy-looking to die for years and years. All right, says he, let's see what can be done. Three and a half millions! That's an incentive for a far more social animal than Skinner. Certainly, it will be Anita's money, but Anita, whatever else she is, is father-dominated to a remarkable extent. You've noticed it? You've seen them together, haven't you? I haven't, but I've seen them separately, and to my mind they fall perfectly into their psychological types. She does what he tells her—she's too frightened not to. He knows he won't have any difficulty in taking all the money he needs from her. Thus he reasons it out, and sets to work. Later, perhaps, he decides that while he is removing Page he may as well settle the Codrington nuisance at the same time, and have a real, slap-up murder mystery to cover himself with. Nobody in their sane senses is going to suspect him, the great scientist. Not for a moment. But he did not expect afterwards to find his daughter so involved with Page, and his secretary so involved with his daughter. Very tiresome, and this evening we have seen how tiresome he is finding it. Doesn't that account for his behaviour?"

"It does; but I can't believe that he—— Dash it, Jupp, you've no more facts to support it than the Inspector has to support his theory!"

"But I've as many, and, obviously, I shall have more."

"How do you know that?"

"Because it is invariably true that a man who sets out to prove a theory always finds the facts he requires. It's dreadful, but, as I say, true. Look at the Pyramid Prophets, look at the Adventists, look at the Freudian psychologists—look at half the people in the world!"

"Yes," I said. "So you're going to set out to prove the Professor is the murderer? Isn't that the same attitude with which the Inspector went after Blake and Anita?"

"Of course it is. But don't you see the immense advantage of having *two* complete cases? Neither will stand unless one considerably outweighs the other in its soundness of evidence, its truth and its justice."

I looked at him, and wondered where his extraordinary brain would lead him before the final stage of the affair was reached.

"And Mendholz?" I asked.

"Whatever Mendholz may have been during the war, to-day he is a piano salesman."

"But his turning up at this time—of all times——"

"Proves it," said Jupp.

CHAPTER IX

ALTHOUGH James Blake had been at "Windy Arbour" for five years, I do not suppose he had been more than three times to the Manor House, and to-night was certainly the first time he had come to dinner with me. I realised as Jeames announced him, and he walked into the drawing-room, that I had missed something in not having got to know him better. When one considered the average dullness of the people I knew at Eastblyth—and I seemed to know them all—people like Page and the Reverend Lionel Lake, it was little short of foolish to have wasted the wit and intelligence of a James Blake. It had surely been my fault, not his. I had a large house and I entertained a certain amount, quite apart from my Lordship of the Manor, which put upon me the onus of making the initial move in such matters. He was not one of your hermit-recluse men at all; he worked hard, and read history in his spare time because that sort of life suited him, but it did not mean that he lacked the gregarious spirit.

I was alone—Jupp was still changing for dinner—and I liked the frankness of his smile as he shook hands. It told me that he appreciated my motive in asking him to Blyth Manor, and that he was in need of companionship—a need which I thoroughly understood. The Professor was up in the air and quite irrational about this murder business, and Anita —well, apart from her dangerous position, there was something else wrong there. I could imagine that there had been somewhat of a scene between her and Blake, and I had half an idea what had caused it. Not Hamish Page's murder, nor yet Lady Codrington's.

I gave him an aperitif, and he said:

"The Professor told me that Mr. Jupp is staying with you. Wasn't he the chap who was with the Inspector this evening?"

"Yes, but he is not of the Inspector's way of thinking," I reassured him.

"Well, that's a relief." He spoke feelingly. "This affair has shaken me, rather, and I was beginning to believe that every man's hand was against me, sort of thing. Panicky, you know. It's a bit frightening, to be suspected of murder, however innocent one may know oneself to be. Which reminds me. For what reason did I kill the unfortunate lady?"

"Because she 'knew too much.'"

"Ah! They have evidence of that?"

"They are looking for it."

He laughed, but not without strain.

"They'll have to look hard."

"They will look hard."

He nodded.

"The might and majesty of the Law."

"You don't mind talking about all this?"

"Good God! I must talk about it! And to somebody sensible like yourself or a George Jupp. The Professor has sent for Critchley-Jenkins. He may come or he may not; in the meantime, I feel I want to get things straightened out. It makes a man think to have a plain-clothes detective following him about the countryside. I came over on a push-bike, and there was some one behind me all the way from the house. . . . I suppose they're afraid I'm going to make a bolt for it!" He laughed again. "I'm not that sort of idiot."

"Stick it out," I agreed. "You've got Jupp believing in you, and although I don't know him very well yet, he strikes me as being a very strong ally to have on one's side—fighting for one."

Jupp came in then, and for the first time I saw him in an almost jovial mood: his gloom and sombreness had entirely left him. Through dinner he kept control of the conversation, and made no attempt to discuss Blake's position. Either it did not appear to him to require discussion, or he saw nothing to be gained by allowing Blake to worry about it. He could not, of course, stop him worrying about it altogether, but he could at least show by his own cheerfulness that he did not regard it as being so serious that a good dinner need be spoilt by it. "Sufficient unto the day" was his attitude, with somewhat of "Better the evil . . ." in it.

Having done his best in this worthy cause, he excused himself after coffee, saying that he was going to call on the Vicar, and left us together. Blake was in much brighter spirits by this time, and I was by way of being grateful to the little detective for having put him in them.

At ten-thirty, after a whisky-and-soda, he said he must go, and thanked me with genuine warmth for what he called my "kindness." We had talked of everything under the sun for the last hour and a half, but we had not once spoken of Anita. Either she was too close to his heart, and in too great a trouble for him to talk about her with comfort, or else he suspected that I was the man she had determined to "get." to use her own word. He may even have known it definitely. Anita was odd. She was quite capable of repulsing him and at the same time confiding in him her ambitions of the moment. Wondering vaguely whether she had done this, I watched him light his bicycle lamp in the porch. There was a faint breeze, and a moon over which small, feathery clouds moved every now and again. I saw a dim figure in the shadow of the box hedge a little way down the drive, and wondered if it was my protecting policeman or Blake's plain-clothes watcher.

We bade one another good-night, and he set off, the bicycle making a soft whirring crunch in the gravel. As his light vanished round the first bend, another bicycle, its lamp alight, emerged from a gap in the box hedge; the man mounted it and followed. The law was not asleep. Although there was no sign on this side of the house of the patrol the Inspector had promised, I was confident that it was somewhere near by.

I went back into the house, and closed the front door. Jupp had not yet put in an appearance, so I turned into the small workshop I had fitted up in a room under the big staircase, where at the moment I had the interior economy of a grandfather clock spread out in jars of paraffin, to be cleaned and repaired in the hope of making it tell the time.

I worked away for half an hour, and about eleven Jupp returned. Jeames let him in, and told him where I was to be found. He came and sat on the corner of the bench, and was apparently relieved to find that Blake had gone. At all events, he gloomed quietly to himself while I scraped the rust of ages from a pinion wheel. I was getting to know him better, and I gathered from his expression of general dissatisfaction that he had spent a profitable evening with the Reverend Lionel Lake.

"Is the Vicar," he said at length, "a really frightful hypocrite?"

"It has been suggested before," I agreed.

He nodded and went on:

"I had no difficulty in persuading him to talk about Lady Codrington. In fact the trouble was to get him to stop. He began about how great a loss her death would prove to have been to English literature. Future generations would deplore her dastardly murder. It seems that he has a great admiration for her work. *The Pipes of the God,* for instance, he claimed to be the greatest study of life under the primitive nature-religions that has ever been done. He attributed no significance to the Home Office ban against its introduction into this country. I can only assume that, in the innocence of his heart, he does not recognise pornography when he reads it. But I wonder? As far as his personal friendship with the authoress was concerned, he somehow gave me the impression that he had been rather successful—as one man of the world to another. He said nothing definite at all; I felt, however, that he wanted me to see him as the bereaved lover who alone of all the world realised the transcendental quality of his mistress: her charm, her generosity, the nobility of her character and the high perfection of her mind. It was a little difficult to realise that he was referring to the poor woman we saw on the heath by Brooker's Mill this afternoon. Presently he set forth upon a theory as to the identity of the person who wrote the forged note. He suggested that there was someone in the neighbourhood at whom the finger of scandal had yet to point, but who had been unable to resist Lady Codrington's physical attractiveness. Not her spiritual attractiveness, which was for the Vicar alone to appreciate. And this person's carnal-mindedness had quite revolted the lady, so that she had repulsed him with contempt and indignation. The reverend gentleman expounded and explained for nearly an hour, and by the end of that time I realised it was indeed the Professor he was referring to, and that although he may have got the facts a bit mixed and distorted, undoubtedly Lady Codrington told him of some fuss or trouble in which the Professor was concerned. In fact the Vicar is a potential witness for the Crown if it comes to a criminal charge being made against Skinner. He can repeat, in short, what the lady told him. At all events I am satisfied, from my point of view, that there was some kind of emotional link between her and the Professor, and further inquiry into it must obviously be made. The Vicar, no doubt set thinking by English's questions about the people who were left alone with his notepaper, cannot forget the unreasonable excuse the Professor had for calling on him the other day so early in the morning. The spoilt view from the bedroom window, if you remember."

"You're talking and reasoning just like the Inspector," I said.

"Of course! If I am to discover a——"

The sound of the front-door bell interrupted him, and the persistence with which it continued to ring suggested considerable urgency. He stopped in mid-sentence, and we looked at each other in mute question.

"I'll open it!" he said, and ran out into the hall as Jeames came through the green baize door which cut off the kitchens. Jeames' eyebrows went up, either because the bell was still ringing or because he disapproved of a guest, even a distinguished detective of a guest, taking upon himself a duty which was obviously the butler's.

Jupp slid back the catch, and cautiously peered through the crack.

"Hullo!" he said, and James Blake strode into the hall. He was wild-eyed and breathless, and his black hair stood straight up from his scalp. He was still in evening clothes, and the ends of his black trousers were dusty. I hurried to meet him.

"*She's gone!*" he cried, and leant against the wall by the door.

"Anita!" I exclaimed.

"Yes! This note—on the ladder up to my room!" He was fighting for breath, and I realised that he must have cycled from "Windy Arbour" at a tremendous speed to have got back so soon. I took the piece of paper from him. At that moment there was an interruption: the large figure of a policeman pushed open the door as Jupp turned to close it.

"Everything all right, sir?" He looked searchingly at Blake.

"Quite, thank you, constable. You're on patrol in the grounds?"

"Yes, sir."

He departed, and I read the pencil-scribbled sentences with which Anita had said good-bye.

"DEAR JIMMY,

"I am going to clear out. There is someone I can go to, and he will look after me. Father is impossible over this business and he frightens me more than that police Inspector. And I can't stick your air of martyrdom. If you had only had the sense to hit me this evening, instead of looking at me like a moonstruck calf and promising to 'stand by' me, I might have stuck it out. But you didn't and I can't. So I am clearing out. Nobody will find me, ever— not even the police. So don't worry. And try to love some-one else; you'll manage it more easily than you think.

"ANITA."

"Where the devil is she going?" Blake cried, and nodded when Jupp asked to see the letter. "Who is she going to?"

"God knows," I said. "She knows so many people."

"She's got to be stopped!" He clenched his fists. "She talks about the police not being able to find her! What a child she is! Doesn't she realise that this dash to get away will be regarded as a confession of guilt? She must be stopped and brought home! Arden, you've got a fast car. She left 'Windy Arbour' about half an hour ago, according to Carstairs, in the car. It hasn't any speed, and it's old. You could catch her up in the Sunbeam before she reaches London. She's certain to make for it: all her—her friends are there."

He looked at me with agonised appeal. Apart from any-thing else, he was right about the opinion the police would form.

"Yes," said Jupp, "she ought to be brought back. What did the Professor say when you told him?"

"I didn't wait to tell him. He couldn't have done anything —except rave—and I hadn't time for that. I came straight to Arden—to suggest the Sunbeam."

Jupp took charge of the situation. He asked Blake to return to "Windy Arbour," and at least make a pretence of going to bed, even if he did not sleep. It would never do for him, in his present position, to be mixed up in whatever the result of our chase might be. There was a man watching him; whether that individual had managed to keep on his trail during his dash back to the Manor House we did not know, but unless he returned at once the neighbourhood would be roused to look for him. In any case there was no reason to suppose that he would be any more use in persuading Anita to return than we would, and we could be trusted to do our best with her. We recognised as clearly as he did that it was utter folly for her to run away.

It took me a bare two minutes to get the Sunbeam out of the garage, and Jupp took his seat beside me. "Right!" he said, and we swung down the drive with a momentary vision of Blake's harassed face in the white beam from the headlights as a farewell benediction.

I have driven by night across the moor to the main Lowestoft to London road on many occasions, but I do not think I ever reached it so soon. The loose stones of the narrow country road scuttled from the swift wheels in a continual rattle against the undersides of the wings, and the engine, quiet though it usually was, drowned our voices.

We turned into the main road, and settled down to a steady fifty miles an hour, which I was able to increase on straight stretches. Saxmundham, in darkness save for a lighted window here and there, passed behind us, and we sped on toward Woodbridge, our headlamps carving a pathway through the night. Trees and bushes by the roadside stood flatly for a moment, without depth, like stage scenery, and vanished to make way for others. The road was empty, for of all the main routes in England I think that particular one, north of Ipswich, carries less traffic than any other. Between Saxmundham and Martlesham one car passed us going in the opposite direction, and we overtook none. A cyclist here and there, as often as not without a light of any description, was all we saw.

Jupp sat quietly, and watched the white ribbon of road unwind before us; only once did he raise his voice above the whistle of air and hum of hard-pressed engine, and then it was to observe:

"She has something over half an hour's start of us, and will perhaps average half this speed, if her car is an old model. We ought to catch up with her somewhere about the thirty-mile mark—assuming she is on this road, and you both seemed to think she would be."

"Whenever she isn't at Eastblyth she's up in town," I shouted in reply. "She's one of those modern young women who believe that the intelligent life is only led in the great big city. 'Intelligent life' means cocktail parties. If she has got a would-be protector in the offing, he'll be there, and nowhere else."

He nodded, and across Martlesham Common, where they have built one of the new wide arterial roads from the aerodrome to the northern outskirts of Ipswich, the speedometer needle wavered past the figure seventy and crept, before I had to slow down for the narrowing of the road at the tram terminus, to seventy-five.

Half-way down the steep Springfield Road, near Mulley's antique shop, I caught sight of a red tail-lamp at the bottom of the hill. Ipswich is just about thirty miles from Eastblyth, and we had been on the road for forty minutes. According to Jupp's mental arithmetic, the car might well be Anita's.

I reached it in the High Street, and passed it, but it was not the dark red two-seater for which we were looking. Ipswich was never built for present-day traffic, and even at midnight, when the streets are empty, it is the kind of town in which one instinctively obeys the speed limit. I suppose it is about a mile long, the worst part, and we emerged on to the Colchester road with a feeling of relief. We shot up the hill on to the plateau at forty-five, and opened out on the level to our former average. The Sunbeam had never behaved better, and I think some of the exhilaration of our speed found its way into Jupp's unenthusiastic consciousness, for I heard him singing a small song to himself.

Two hundred yards this side of the A.A. control at the fork-roads five miles beyond Ipswich, where the red beacon light winks tirelessly through the hours of darkness, we came up with Anita. I had pressed her into the hedge, to her vehement and vituperative disgust, before she realised who we were and could do anything about it. I drew up alongside the two-seater, and the Sunbeam's engine quietened to a restful, silken whisper as I took my stiff foot from the throttle-pedal.

"Anita," I said, "you're coming back at once."

"*John!*" she cried, and but for Jupp's presence I felt there would have been another note in her voice besides mere surprise.

"I won't!" she added. "How dare you chase me like this!"

Her face was a dim white blurr in the reflected light from the headlamps.

"Do you want to die?" I asked. "Do you want to be hanged by your slim neck until you are dead? Because you are behaving in exactly the best way to bring that about. You've got a cowardly streak in you, and you're letting it run you."

"I haven't! I'm not!"

"A cowardly streak," I repeated. "You're proposing to let Blake bear the brunt of your own stupidities. You've involved him, and you've got to help get him out."

"I didn't ask the fool to fall in love with me. I was only flirting with him, and if he hadn't been such a poor fish he would have known it."

"If he had been as light as yourself, you mean. I tell you frankly, Anita, if you don't turn that car round and drive back to Eastblyth I'll take you back."

"You—you couldn't!"

"I could. I would tie you hand and foot, and gag you if it seemed necessary. I'm in earnest, Anita. You're not going to be allowed to run away. For once in your selfish life, you are going to sit up and take your medicine like a decent being."

"Oh, damn you! Damn you!" she said. "You don't know what you're asking me to do! They want to pin these murders on me!" Her voice rose to a wail. "And I didn't do them! I don't know who did, and I don't care. But I can't stand the suspense, the waiting—that policeman! He wants to see me in a cell, where I can't get out!"

Jupp spoke for the first time since we had stopped.

"Pull yourself together, Miss Skinner!" His tone was needle-sharp. "You aren't going to be hanged, but if you persist in this folly you'll come near to it. I can assure you of that."

She was silent for a moment, fighting against a hysteria of fear.

"All right," she said finally.

Jupp got into the seat by her side, and she backed and turned the two-seater. I followed suit with the Sunbeam, and, with Anita leading, drove back along the road by which we had come. Either Jupp explained the advantage it would be if she could get home to "Windy Arbour" before someone discovered her flight, or else she was in that mood of desperation for which speed seems an antidote, for I found that she was pushing the two-seater along at a pace which could not have been good for it.

At about twenty minutes past one we turned on to the familiar Eastblyth moor. At the place where the lane branched off to Inderswick, Anita stopped, and waited for me to come up. I drew up abreast of her, the running boards almost touching.

"I want to ask you a favour, John," she said. "May I stay at the Manor to-night? I can't bear the thought of trying to sleep —up there." She made a slight gesture of her shoulder towards the hill, where the roofs of "Windy Arbour" were outlined against the night sky. "Honestly, John, I'm all in—I——"

She just stretched out her hand and touched mine, where it rested on the Sunbeam's wheel. Her fingers were cold after her two hours' driving.

"Please let me," she said. "You would, if you knew how frightened I was."

I tried to see Jupp's face, but there wasn't enough light.

"What about Blake?" I said. "He's worrying his head off about you, wondering if we have found you."

"Oh, bother him!" she cried. "It's Blake, Blake, Blake all the time! I hate the very sound of his stupid name! Let him worry! But I won't go back to-night—in the morning I promise I will——"

I thought for a moment.

"As you wish," I said.

I called up "Windy Arbour" on the telephone the moment we got in. After an interval the Professor answered it. I told him briefly that Anita was in a state of nervous anxiety about things, and wanted to stay the night at the Manor. She was here now, and Mrs. Jeames would look after her. Would he please tell Blake, who was worried about her?

"The devil he is!" snapped the Professor irritably. "I can't think why anybody bothers with the wretched girl! Here— Jimmy!" His voice receded as he called to the young man.

Apparently they were both up. Actually the Professor had had an idea, and had insisted upon getting to work on it at once, with Blake's help. Blake explained this when he came to the telephone. He was very grateful for the news that we had managed to stop Anita and bring her back, but to the information that she had decided to stay at the Manor for the night he brought no enthusiasm at all. He said, "Oh!" rather blankly, and bade me good night. The instrument clicked, and I hung up the receiver. Jupp was out of the room, and Anita was listening to my end of the conversation. At the abrupt finish to it, which she had no difficulty in realising, she laughed with faint amusement.

"Jimmy's frantically jealous of you."

"Yes?"

"Dramatically the other day he demanded to know the name of the 'some other man' who made it impossible for me to care for him."

"So you told him that I occupied that happy position, I suppose.

"Well, it was perfectly true—then. I'm not sure what I should say if he were to ask me the same question now. You've been rather harsh with me, you know, considering everything. I'm not one of your noble, self-sacrificing heroines."

"No," I agreed. "In fact you're barely human. You let a decent, honest person like Blake throw his heart at your feet—you know you could have stopped him if you had wanted to—and then laugh at him!"

"Why should I stop him?" she cut in. "It was one of the most entertaining experiences I've had for months and months!"

I was more than relieved that Jupp returned at that moment, and attacked the whisky decanter. A moment later, and he might have found me with Anita's throat between my hands, conducting the third Eastblyth murder. She was not fit to continue her existence.

Actually it was terminated that same night between the hours of three and four a.m.

Mrs. Jeames, taking a cup of early tea to the blue guest room at about the same time that Hamish Page's valet had taken tea to his master three mornings previously at the Towers, found Anita Skinner lying in a heap at the wide-open window.

She was stone dead, with a small clean hole in her forehead.

CHAPTER X

MRS. JEAMES dropped the tray of tea-things and screamed—screamed twice. The sound quivered and resounded through the house, and I reached the door of my room as she came running down the passage with her face as lacking in colour as her apron.

"Oh, sir! The young lady——!" she cried, and incontinently

collapsed in my arms in a dead faint. I lowered her to the floor, for she is of that build which is euphemistically called "comfortable." Shouting to Jeames, whom I could hear in the hall below, to come and attend to her, I hurried to the blue room. The door was open as the housekeeper had left it in her panic to summon me, and because the window was open also, the morning breeze was able to blow through the room. The still body, clad in a pair of pink-and-white silk pyjamas which were too large, lay on the polished oak floor below the sill.

I did not go in, but crossed the landing into the main part of the house, where Jupp was sleeping. He had heard the clatter of the dropped tray and the housekeeper's screams, and was emerging from his door as I turned into the corridor to summon him. He was tying the girdle of a brilliant scarlet dressing-gown which Sherlock Holmes would have envied.

"They've killed Anita," I said briefly.

"My God!" he said, and accompanied me to the blue room. "They have——"

We stepped over the broken crockery and steaming pool of tea, and crossed to where the body lay. Jupp bent down and put his hand on the shoulder.

"Hours ago," he said, straightening himself, and looked at the Chippendale clock on the mantelshelf. "Eight-fifteen. Make a note of the time. Now we must ring up the Inspector. You speak to him. It's your house——"

We went downstairs to the telephone, and I got on to the Station-sergeant. I told him what had happened, and he said he would send across to the Inspector at once. In the meantime would I please take care that neither the body nor anything else in the room was touched? I would.

"The person I want to see is the constable who was on duty in the grounds," said Jupp. "Let's look for him. Just a moment, though. I want to take another look round her room before English gets here. We'll be very careful not to touch anything. The Law must be obeyed."

I went up with him, and watched his swift but comprehensive examination. It was obvious that Anita had got out of bed and gone to the window: she had thrown back the bed-clothes, and the fashion in which they lay suggested nothing of what her thoughts or emotions had been at the time. There was a certain amount of coagulated blood on the floor by the head, showing that at the moment of death she must have been at or very near the place where her body now lay. The last heart-beats had forced the blood through the broken vessels of the wounds caused by the bullet, for as Jupp pointed out to me, there was in this case, unlike those of Hamish Page and Lady Codrington, a complete penetration, entrance and exit, of the skull, the bullet having emerged cleanly from the parietal bone. He indicated the spot, and asked me if I saw anything significant about it.

"I see what you mean," I said. "Nickel-plated bullet? The usual soft-lead ·22 would spread out after its force had been checked by its entrance, and, if it came out at all, would make more of a—more of a hole?"

"Exactly," he said. "And if she was shot from the outside, there's quite a chance that we shall find the bullet somewhere in the room—it certainly isn't in the head still——"

We searched for the bullet, and did not find it. Jupp became silent, and looked out of the window for several moments in deep thought. He walked to the door, peered at the dis-tempered wall on either side of it, examined the door itself, and finally shrugged his shoulders. There was no sign of the bullet.

We left the room, and I locked the door, taking the key. Jupp's silence affected me, and I felt no desire to discuss the affair or ask questions. The mood was dispelled in a certain measure by the difficulty we had in getting Mrs. Jeames down the stairs into the haven of her own apartments. We managed it somehow, and Jupp and I went out into the garden. After shouting "Hi!" and "Officer!" the constable whom we had seen last night when Blake returned with the news of Anita's effort to run away came out of the rose pergola. He seemed sleepy, to my way of thinking. He saluted.

Jupp tackled him at once.

"Everything quiet during the night, officer?"

"Yes, sir. As peaceful as you like."

"You didn't see anybody?"

"Not a soul, sir." He was vaguely puzzled.

"Hear anything?"

"No, sir."

"What time did we get back after our motor drive?"

"One twenty-eight, sir." He had observed that event, at any rate.

"You're taking turn and turn about with another man, I suppose?"

"Yes, sir. Two hours on, two hours off right through. P.C. Greene is with me. He's off now, and sleeping in the gardener's shed at the moment—we've fixed up a kind of a couch in there."

"Good idea! Did P.C. Greene see or hear anything?"

"Not that he told me of, sir. Is there anything wrong? Has somethin' happened, sir?"

"A lady was shot some time during the night while she was standing at that window up there," said Jupp.

The constable was a young man, and his chin-strap supported his slackening jaw.

"Crummy!" he muttered, and stared at the window. He pulled himself together.

"Shot, sir? Not murdered like the other two?"

"Yes."

I gave him the key of the blue room, assured him that the door was safely locked, and that we had summoned the Inspector, and left him to awaken his colleague, Greene. Jupp sneezed, for the autumn morning was cool, and we went into the house.

"There was a heavy dew last night," he observed. "And we may find signs of the murderer on the grass or in the bushes —except that two policemen have been walking about all night, which won't make it any easier. *If* they walked about——"

"You mean, how did the murderer approach near enough to get Anita to the window and shoot her without being either seen or heard by them?"

"Quite! A matter which the Inspector will have to decide. They are his men."

We observed that we wanted food, apart from the fact that it was about breakfast time. I noticed during the war that danger or excitement, or indeed any kind of strain, will make a man hungry at a time when theoretically the thought of eating should be far from him. So we attacked a plate of fruit on the sideboard in the dining-room, and waited for the Inspector. Neither of us had shaved or bathed, but neither of us wanted to miss his reactions to this the third murder. Jupp was shaken. There was nothing gloomy in his expression now, but instead, a strange, vulpine intentness. He munched a Cox's orange pippin, and stared continuously for a space of minutes into the garden, where the green of lawns and trees was powdered with grey dew. The pale gold of a rising sun shone upon the tranquil world.

"Oh, damn this!" he remarked suddenly. Then we heard the heavy feet of a policeman as he climbed the stairs to guard the door behind which the dead girl lay.

"One thing is clear," Jupp added, with more firmness of tone. "We can't begin to work on this case until we have collected a number of ascertainable facts."

"For instance?"

"Detailed reports of the two policemen who were on duty here, of the plain-clothes man at 'Windy Arbour' and of any other of the Inspector's representatives there may have been in the immediate neighbourhood of the two places."

"You think the murderer came from 'Windy Arbour'?"

"Apart from the fact that the two favourite theories of the moment have their suspects there, we cannot escape the almost certain truth that the poor girl's presence here was known only to the members of the Skinner household besides ourselves."

"Lord!" I muttered. "That *is* true! Unless the murderer was hanging about this garden, and saw us bring her home last night. That was my first assumption."

"Why, if he was going to murder her, did he hang round

here instead of 'Windy Arbour'? Does she often spend the night here?"

"I see. Never before. To be perfectly frank, it occurred to me almost immediately that the fellow, whoever he is, was out gunning for *me*. Anita, for some reason, afforded him a better chance, and he took it. She was one of the dinner-party, and although I cannot explain *why*, three of the people who were present at it have been killed—murdered. I also cannot ignore the mathematics of the fact. Three! And none outside the circle of that particular gathering. It seems to me there must be an underlying significance somewhere— it's beyond the numerical likelihood of coincidence. You see what I mean——? Three out of the six——"

He was looking at me keenly.

"You are no longer considering the alibi theory of the attempt on you? There hasn't been another, has there? Like there was on Page—a successful attempt?"

I shrugged my shoulders, and took another nectarine.

"I have just suggested that the murderer came last night to have another bang at me," I said, "and saw Anita arrive. He may even have failed to get me to the window, but succeeded with her.

"For God's sake, then, what is the motive?" he demanded. "The motive which makes the murder of the four of you profitable? Page, Lady Codrington, Anita and yourself? Tell me that, if you include yourself in the plan and ambitions of this fiend!"

"I'm damned if I can!" I said.

"All right," he muttered sulkily. "Leave yourself out of it, but add the Vicar and Professor Skinner to your list. Are you anticipating that they too will——"

"Here is the Inspector," I interrupted.

A two-seater containing the Inspector, Dr. Allis and Sergeant Grice came up the drive and stopped at the front door. Like ourselves, English was rather less spruce than usual, and I suspected from the blueness of his chin that he, too, had not shaved. His eyes were very anxious.

We told him briefly how Mrs. Jeames had come upon the tragedy, and how we had locked the door and telephoned for him.

"Quite right," he said shortly. "Take me up. Come, doctor. Grice, take charge of things down here, and have Roberts and Greene ready for me."

"One of them is upstairs, I think," I said. "I gave Roberts the key of the room."

"Hope he's not meddling," he remarked, and we went up the stairs in a bunch. The constable was outside the blue room, and he handed the Inspector the key.

Ten minutes sufficed him to come, with Dr. Allis' assistance, to the obvious conclusions.

"Dead three to five hours; bullet through the brain, no possibility of a *felo-de-se* . . . killed while she stood at the window—death instantaneous. Nickel-plated bullet, same kind as the one which killed Page—no sign of it in the room —probably ricochetted out into the garden again. I'll have a more extensive search made for it, though."

I exchanged a glance with Jupp. The autopsy on the millionaire had produced a nickel-plated bullet.

The body was carried to the bed and put on it. A sheet was drawn over it. We went out on to the landing.

"Now, Mr. Arden," said the Inspector. "How did Miss Skinner come to sleep the night here? It must have been rather an unexpected arrangement. I see she had no night-clothes of her own with her."

I told him, as accurately as possible, the details of the incident of the previous night.

"So that was why Blake came back here, was it?" he commented, showing us that he had already had some kind of a report from the shadow who was watching the young man.

"We agreed with Blake," put in Jupp, "that she must not be allowed to absent herself from Eastblyth at such a time."

English nodded.

"So she was nervous of returning to 'Windy Arbour'? Did she say why?"

"She said something about her father being in an ill-humour with her—something to that effect," I said.

"Surely that did not sound a very plausible excuse."

"It did not occur to me to doubt it at the time."

"She was frightened of going home; we'll leave it at that."

I thought of Jupp's shrewd remark yesterday. The Inspector was looking for facts to fit his particular predelictions. Neither of us had suggested that Anita had been actually "frightened," and yet it might be called another word for "nervous" or even "disinclined." Fear may have been her real reason. And, according to the Inspector, fear of James Blake, who had shown such determination not to allow her to escape. And why had he been so determined? Naturally because he realised that her knowledge of his activities during the last week would be terribly dangerous to him if she gave it to the police, and she might do that if he was not near her to see that she held her tongue.

One could watch the Inspector's mind working. Blake had had as good, indeed a better motive for murdering Anita, than he had had for murdering the others. Her attempt to escape had told him, as surely as if she had confessed to him in words, that she had not the courage to face the stringent inquiry which must inevitably come, and just as he had dared not let her pass out of his sight, so he had decided he dared not let her live. Before he knew what was happening she would turn King's Evidence, and send him to the gallows.

"Tell me," said English. "Did you let them know at 'Windy Arbour' that she was staying the night?"

"Yes. I spoke to her father on the 'phone."

"Professor Skinner. To no one else?"

"Blake, of course. He had to be told that we had brought her safely back."

I saw the expression of "Ah, I told you so!" come into his keen eyes.

"Now Roberts." And he questioned him, and afterwards P.C. Greene, about the events of the night. The result was disappointing. Short of accusing them of sleeping at their posts, he could not come to any definite conclusion as to how the murderer had managed to evade their notice both in sight and sound.

"A rifle of this calibre," he explained, "used with a silencer of the usual type, say a Maxim, makes a noise rather like the dull clap of gloved hands. It can be heard quite clearly at a distance of say thirty yards."

"Provided there is no wind to carry the sound away from you, or the rustle and creak of tree branches to obscure it," remarked Jupp, and the Inspector made a gesture of impatience.

"Did either of you men hear a sound like that?" he asked the constables.

They would have liked to hear it, if only to please him, but manifestly they hadn't.

"Did you?" he inquired of Jupp and me.

"Personally," I said, "I slept soundly after driving those sixty odd miles. In fact I think that under ordinary circumstances I might have heard at least the fall of the body. My room is in the same wing as the blue guest room, and at the end of the same passage. The doors, of course, were shut."

"Who else sleeps in the same wing?"

"The servants, but on the floor above."

"Nobody on your floor?"

"Jupp, but he was on the other side of this landing and down the corridor. Strictly speaking, that is the main portion of the house, not what we call the west wing."

"I see. We'll have the servants in the hall downstairs, if you please, Mr. Arden. I want to discover, if possible, the time the shot was fired. It is always of enormous help to have that."

He drew Sergeant Grice aside and spoke to him. The sergeant departed briskly, and I realised that he was going to "Windy Arbour" to hold James Blake safely until the Inspector got there.

While the interrogation of the servants was in progress Jupp and I made hurried toilets, and learnt when we descended again that nothing had been discovered. No unusual sound or circumstance had disturbed the household. Jeames testified to the undisturbed condition that morning of the locks, bolts and shutters which he had closed and fastened the night before.

"Were you still up when Mr. Arden, Mr. Jupp and Miss Skinner arrived home at half-past one?"

"Of course, sir. Mr. Arden had instructed me to wait, in case he needed anything when he returned."

The Inspector then conducted, with the aid of the constables, a brief but careful examination of the house, which produced no fact of significance. The three of us went into the lounge together, and closed the door.

"Presumably Professor Skinner does not know yet?" English asked.

"None of us has communicated with him."

He nodded.

"An unpleasant task for me."

"I'll tell him," said Jupp.

"Do you want to, particularly?" The Inspector flung a quick, shrewd glance at him. "What are you after, Mr. Jupp?"

"The murderer."

"Of course. But I mean as far as the Professor's concerned? Whenever you say anything, or ask a question, I've noticed he is somewhere in it."

"I'm interested in him. He's a strange type. I want to see what he says and does when he is told his daughter has been murdered."

"You expect him to give someone away?"

"He might—it's conceivable."

"He knows more than we do, you think?"

"Mm."

"I may as well tell you," said English after a pause, "that this new horror has upset my theory a bit. I don't see how Blake can have come over here during the night without being followed by my man. I've had him watched, you see, and he could not have done the shooting without being held up. However, I'm going over to 'Windy Arbour' at once, and we'll soon see where we stand." He started for the door.

"Was your man watching the Professor too?" asked Jupp. The Inspector stopped.

"The Professor *again*! Of course he wasn't watching the Professor. Why should he?"

"Personally," said Jupp gloomily, "I should have been more comfortable if he had been."

"Do you suspect the Professor of killing his own daughter?" cried English in consternation.

"Well, he could have killed both Hamish Page and Lady Codrington quite easily. For that matter, why suspect Blake of killing the woman he loved?"

The Inspector stared. He realised that Jupp was preparing to talk instead of merely asking questions, and although he thought the famous detective had taken leave of his senses, he could not afford to ignore whatever he wanted to say, however much in a hurry he himself might be to get to "Windy Arbour" and a more fruitful field of inquiry.

"This is a very serious business," he told Jupp. "The country —the Press—was in a sufficient state of excitement yesterday, and I had to issue a statement last night—had to. I said that an arrest was likely—you see, I expected to be able to charge James Blake immediately after the inquest this afternoon. I may yet be able to. But in any case this third murder within three days is going to set the whole civilised world shouting for police action, and something has got to be done. I tell you frankly that I consider the evidence against Blake in the first two cases to be sufficient to have justified my applying for the warrant. I have it in my pocket. Mr. Jupp, I have a great respect for your abilities, but I assure you you will find me hard to convince of any theory which tries to show that Blake had nothing to do with the murders of Mr. Page and Lady Codrington. Of this Anita Skinner killing we know little as yet, but the advantage of her death to that young man in his present position is tremendous. She shared his guilt; she was a potential witness against him. He was afraid of what we might learn from her."

Jupp nodded.

"Fear can outweigh all other human emotions. It is, of course, the thing from which all human emotion springs, if you go deep enough."

The Inspector became impatient.

"Have you anything new to tell me, Mr. Jupp?"

"The Vicar has a story about a liaison between Professor Skinner and victim Number Two."

"Lady Codrington? Is it authenticated?"

"It might bear looking into."

I saw that Jupp had realised how impossible it would be to get the Inspector to see eye to eye with him about the Professor. The theory of "The Silent Skinner" was ingenious, but lacked evidence; the Professor's probable motives for murder were in all three cases less powerful than those attributable to Blake. One could not escape it. I knew that Jupp had realised the moment he saw Anita's body that in the Professor he had not as likely a murderer as had English in James Blake. If he was going to persuade the Inspector that Blake was innocent, he would have to produce something more satisfying, something rather startling.

Looking back on that moment, I think he was beginning to catch a glimpse of the true explanation, if not to realise the identity of the real murderer. I cannot be sure, although in so much of the rest of the case I was able to keep in touch with his mind, as it were, and almost anticipate what he would think next—a vastly interesting experience for me.

He saw then, however, that nothing in the world could save James Blake from arrest. Indeed, he may have thought it an advantage, in that it would put the poor man out of his misery of suspense and enable him, with Critchley-Jenkins' assistance, to form a stout defence to meet the case for the Crown. Whether or not, of course, it could be suggested that he was responsible for Anita's death, Jupp did not yet know, but because Blake had not killed her was not necessarily proof that he had not killed the millionaire and Lady Codrington.

The shooting of Anita Skinner, it might be claimed, was possibly the work of another and separate murderer who was innocent of the first two deaths, but who had made use of the same method in order to escape detection. The only serious objections to that theory, however, lay in the detail of the nickel-plated bullets. Page—we did not know yet about Lady Codrington—had been killed by the same type of bullet as the one which had passed through the girl's brain; an unusual type.

I was brought to this train of thought by a statement and a question to which Jupp restricted his argument with Inspector English. He said:

"If Blake shot Anita Skinner, he must have used a weapon you have not yet found. Those cartridges you took from 'Windy Arbour' with the rifles, were they nickel-covered?"

The Inspector smiled grimly.

"They were!" he said.

"What?" I cried.

They both looked at me, Jupp in spite of his surprise. He had not expected that answer to his question.

"It's particularly damning, that," I explained. "Nickel-plated bullets are four or five times the price of the ordinary kind. One doesn't use them for sinking old tins in the sea. At least, I wouldn't."

"You wouldn't unless you were the assistant of an armament expert—with cartridges and what-not lying about the place," observed Jupp. "Do you remember what Blake said yesterday when he was talking about his target-shooting? He referred to a recent expedition to sink tins as 'using up a couple of hundred cartridges.' *Using up.*"

"You haven't done the autopsy on Lady Codrington yet?" I asked.

"Dr. Allis is going to do that this morning. Mr. Jupp, I know you like the look of that young man, but you'll have to make up your mind to this: he killed Mr. Hamish Page, and he killed Lady Codrington. As to the third, this terrible affair of the girl—for she was younger and she was his friend—his accomplice, if you like, someone to stand by—as to this one, we know next to nothing as yet. But if you'll come over to 'Windy Arbour' with me——"

He paused. There was a knock at the door, and Roberts, the constable, entered. He was slightly excited.

"Excuse me, Inspector, but I've found that bullet. In that puddle of tea it was, by the door."

The Inspector took the small, bright piece of metal carefully between forefinger and thumb.

"That's the fellow!" he said. "It's scarcely distorted at all."

"It's very clean," observed Jupp gloomily.

"It's had a pot of hot tea spilt on it—don't forget that. We never thought of looking in that mess of broken crockery. Thanks, Roberts."

Roberts saluted with a gratified expression, probably feeling that his discovery of the bullet had to some extent atoned for his failure to hear the dull clap of gloved hands which was presumed to have accompanied its firing. He left us.

The Inspector put the exhibit carefully away in his pocket case. We went to "Windy Arbour" and the strange facts which awaited us there.

CHAPTER XI

Dr. Allis went back to Southwold in the car in which they had arrived; Jupp volunteered to drive home the Professor's two-seater, which we had put in the Manor garage last night, while I took Inspector English and P.C. Greene in the Sunbeam. The Inspector sat beside me and did not speak until we came to the Professor's private road, when he said:

"Sergeant Grice was to find Walters, and meet me here, at this gate, at nine-fifteen. It's twenty past."

It was nearer twenty-five past according to the dashboard clock, which keeps excellent time. There was certainly no sign of the two policemen anywhere near the gate.

"Shall I stop?" I said, but he asked me to continue on to the house.

Sergeant Grice met us. He emerged alone from the trees on the right-hand side of the drive at a point halfway up it, near where we had first seen the plain-clothes man. I stopped the car level with him.

"I can't find Walters, sir," he told the Inspector. "He must be about somewhere, but I suppose I've missed him. I went all round the edge of the garden, and up to the wall round the courtyard." He was a bit puzzled.

"Is everything quiet up at the house?"

"I didn't notice that it wasn't, sir, although I did not take any definite steps toward ascertaining the state of things there. I was too busy looking for Walters."

"Seen anybody?"

"Not a soul, sir, except the butler. He opened a window on the ground floor, south side, when I was round that way, and I caught a glimpse of his face for a moment."

"It's near breakfast time—I daresay they're at table now," commented the Inspector. "Walters is somewhere about. Jump in, Grice. Mr. Arden will give you a lift. Straight to the door, Mr. Arden, please."

Carstairs opened it for us, and was startled by the sight of so many policemen.

"The Professor's out," he said. "He left for London at eight o'clock." To me he added: "Good morning, sir."

"London!" muttered the Inspector, and frowned. He had not yet realised the Professor's capacity for detachment.

"Once a month," volunteered Carstairs, "he goes to London for the day, on business. Sometimes he stays the night."

"Perfectly true," I said.

"Mr. Blake will be coming across from the workshop any minute now; he's late as it is," the butler informed us. "If you'd like to see him about—er—about whatever it is—he's the Professor's secretary and assistant," Carstairs added. He did not know what this visit portended, but he wanted to badly.

English nodded briskly.

"Please tell him I am here and wish to see him. Just a moment though, before you go. The Professor worked late last night, I believe?"

Carstairs, already surprised, became vaguely apprehensive.

"Until nearly two o'clock, sir."

"You had not gone to bed?"

"Oh yes, sir, but I was late getting off to sleep. I heard him come up to his room. Excuse me, sir, but has anything—happened?"

The Inspector apparently did not hear this question.

"Mr. Blake worked with him until two?"

"I expect so, sir."

"Why do you expect he did?"

"Well, he usually does—whatever the time of day or night it is. The Professor relies on him a lot."

"I see. You don't *know* Mr. Blake went to bed at two?"

"No, sir, I don't. There's no way I could know. He sleeps over number one workshop, and he's quite away from the rest of the house."

"Quite. You knew Miss Skinner was not returning last night?"

"I knew she went out about eleven, and I did not hear her return. It was not until this morning that the master told me she had stayed over at the Manor."

"Has a Mr. Walters called here this morning—or during the night?"

"A Mr. Walters? No, sir. No one's called: you're the first —er—visitors. During the *night*, sir? Dear me, no!"

"All right. Tell Mr. Blake I'm here, would you, please?"

"Will you wait in the lounge while I fetch him? He may be a moment or two, if he hasn't dressed. Being late last night, no doubt he has slept on a bit—and knowing there isn't so much work to-day, the Professor being in Town."

We waited in the lounge, in rather grim silence, for several minutes before Carstairs reappeared. He wore a puzzled expression.

"Mr. Blake isn't over there, sir. I'll look upstairs. He may have gone up to the bathroom without my seeing——"

But Mr. Blake hadn't. Mr. Blake, in fact, had disappeared. The butler was genuinely surprised when he realised that it was so. He went into the kitchen and interviewed the servants.

Nobody in the house had seen Mr. Blake.

"Perhaps he went up to Town with the Professor," I suggested. "He does sometimes."

"Not to-day he didn't, sir." Carstairs was positive about it. He had personally seen the Professor into the car which took him to the station. Whose car? the Inspector wanted to know. The car from Rogers' garage. As a rule, if Miss Anita or Mr. Blake didn't drive him to Darsham station in the two-seater, he ordered a car from Rogers by telephone. This morning, of course, the two-seater had not been available. The Professor had been a bit irritable about it—he'd gone off in a hurry— and—a scurry, rather, being anxious not to miss the eight-twenty.

The Inspector became active. The whole lot of us—Carstairs, Jupp, Sergeant Grice, the constable and myself—were set to searching for Blake and, secondarily, for Walters, the detective. I kept by Jupp, who remarked:

"It looks as though Blake has gone off somewhere and Walters is sticking to him, obeying the Inspector's instructions."

"I wonder what time he started?" I said.

He shrugged his shoulders.

"His bed up there appears to have been slept in. That's all we know for certain. Nobody has seen him at all this morning. Unless the Professor did, and he isn't here to tell us whether he did. The Professor isn't here. Why isn't he here?"

"He goes up once——"

"I know he does. But why did he go *to-day*? He didn't say anything about it yesterday, did he? And do you remember how Blake told the Inspector he would 'do his best' to be at the police-station to-day to make that statement? He meant 'do his best' in view of the Professor's irritation with the inquiry and his insistence that he had a lot of work to do in which Blake was to help him. Blake wouldn't have anticipated being prevented from seeing the Inspector if he had known the Professor was going up to London, would he?"

"He would not, I say, taking the Inspector's view for the purpose of argument, but equally reasonable is it to suppose

124

that the Professor didn't know himself he was going until this morning. We know what Skinner is like—at least, I do. He's exactly the man to wake up at half-past seven, decide before his eyes are properly open to go to Town, and catch the eight-twenty. It's the train he invariably travels by; and there's a breakfast car on it."

Jupp made a furious gesture.

"This horrible affair is talk, talk, talk—*murder*! Talk, talk, talk—*murder*! And then more talk, and a few more mysterious circumstances. It is somewhat idiotic to point it out, it's so obvious, but we haven't got the beginning of an idea where to begin looking for the murderer."

"For Blake, you mean?"

"Stop being the Inspector, for God's sake! It's bad enough to have to contend with the real one!"

We made a complete exploration of the garden and the belt of oak trees which sheltered it from the sea winds. Occasionally we shouted the names of the missing men. The Inspector chose a time when everyone was out of the way to search Blake's rooms, a bedroom and a sitting-room, which occupied the upper story of the workshop nearer the house. This revealed neither ·22 silenced rifle nor secret store of nickel-plated bullets, but it produced a number of interesting documents, not least amongst which was the octet of a sonnet in which the name "Anita" appeared twice. Apparently it was of quite recent composition, for it was lying on top of other pages on the desk in the sitting-room. If it did nothing else for the Inspector, it proved conclusively to him that the couple had been on very intimate terms indeed. He had the good taste merely to hand it to the coroner that afternoon, instead of having it read out in court. The girl was dead—murdered—and Blake was fighting for his life by then. Time enough for the distressing intimacies when the trial began. On or in the desk he also found a collection of unpaid bills and what are termed "pressing" letters. The bills were mostly from firms such as glass-blowers, scientific instrument-makers and wholesale drug houses, and for quite large sums. One gathered that, like the Professor, the young man sometimes had the bright idea which permitted him neither respite nor rest until it was expressed in practical demonstration.

These, as evidence of Blake's need for money, for a wealthy marriage, the Inspector left for the moment on the desk, together with the unfinished sonnet, but he locked the door and pocketed the key. He told us briefly but triumphantly what he had found, and personally joined in the search. He was, he said, frankly anxious. It was very unlike Walters neither to have left word nor sent a message to say that he might be taken far afield. It looked suspiciously as though Blake had made a serious effort to escape, and by his speed and unexpectedness of departure and progress had made it impossible for the detective to inform headquarters.

I gathered from this that some pre-arranged system of communication had broken down.

Carstairs produced a housemaid whose bedroom window overlooked the workshop; she had been awake with toothache between three and four a.m. and had noticed a light burning in Mr. Blake's bedroom for about fifteen minutes about half-way through that period. That was all she had noticed; no, the courtyard and the workshop door were not visible from her room. She had not heard anything. Had she seen that light in his room any other night? No. The Inspector concealed his disappointment, and turned his attention to the telephone—this was about five minutes to ten—and rang up several neighbouring police-stations—Darsham, Saxmundham, Halesworth—in the hope of learning that they had heard from Walters. But they had not. He gave instructions that he was to be looked for, and also a man of the following description—he described James Blake—who was wanted for murder.

It gave me an uncomfortable feeling to hear that phrase. I could not get Blake's dark, anxious face out of my mind; he was so tremendously innocent of the crimes they sought to lay at his door. The chain of circumstances, drawn tighter by every new fact, surrounded and enveloped him. And now, at its end, came his disappearance, which I could not bring myself to believe was deliberate. He had realised as clearly as Jupp and I the foolishness of Anita's attempt to escape; surely he would not make the very mistake he had been instrumental in preventing her from making? And yet I saw the logic of the Inspector's reasoning. Apart from the fact the woman he loved was now dead, and probably by his hand, thus making flight a relief and an apparent safety, it was easy to believe that what he had seen as folly in Anita had assumed wisdom in himself. Desperate with the guilt and the knowledge that the police were about to arrest him, he had determined to destroy with one bullet the girl he had lost and the chief witness against him.

"He was awake between three and four," said English. "A light was seen in his room. Between those hours Miss Skinner was killed."

He shrugged his shoulders, and added:

"Walters may have followed him to the Manor House garden, and watched him elude the patrolling constables—he may even have seen the shot fired, although I doubt that. Obviously he would have realised what was about to happen, and interfered. On the other hand, Blake may have left his rooms and the workshop without Walters realising it, and only quite recently Walters has discovered he has gone. He may be trying to establish contact with him even now."

Jupp offered no theory, but he asked a question.

"Are you going to try to get in touch with the Professor in London, Inspector, and ask him when he is coming back?"

"Don't you think he is coming back?"

"He seems rather an uncertain kind of man—he may decide to stay a fortnight."

"The butler says he'll be back either to-night or to-morrow morning."

"Well, I daresay he will when he sees in the papers what has happened to his daughter. He inherits as next-of-kin about three and a half million pounds."

"Eh?" said the Inspector sharply.

"He does, doesn't he? The lawyer, Snarlett, was a bit firm

with Miss Skinner about her not having any rights to the property until the Will was proved, but he never suggested for a moment that it wouldn't be. I think you will find it's legally water-tight. And since she wasn't killed until after Page's death there's no question of the estate reverting to any secondary legatee, is there? I mean, the fortune is safely in the Skinner family, even if the girl is no longer alive to enjoy it."

"Mr. Jupp," retorted English with great firmness, "I can't bring myself to share your suspicions of Professor Skinner."

"No? Well, I feel it's a pity—not because I'm ready to stake my reputation that the Professor is the guilty man, but because I'm *almost* ready to stake it that young Blake isn't."

The Inspector regarded him with exasperation for a moment, and then with an expression which suggested that even the most infallible of us occasionally make mistakes. It might be that the famous criminologist was wrong, while a Suffolk inspector of police was right. But for the necessity of the moment for constructive action of some kind he might have sat down and argued the point with his valuable if un-official colleague—the necessity, however, was clearly there.

He collected Carstairs, and taking him up to Blake's bed-room, asked him to decide by an examination of his wardrobe how the young man was likely to be dressed at the present moment. The butler, now fully awakened to the significance of the occasion, succeeded in arriving at a conclusion which satisfied the Inspector. Dark grey flannel suit and a soft felt hat—he always wore that kind, usually with a flat brim slightly up at the back and down in front. Carstairs, however, could not decide the colour of the shoes, but thought that they were probably brown, since a grey suit was being worn. The question of whether he had taken a light grey overcoat or a fawn rainproof was settled in favour of the latter, since there was only one on the peg, and he possessed two.

Thus a description was decided upon, and while the entire staff, house and outdoor, continued to search under Sergeant Grice, the Inspector once again made use of the telephone, and circulated to his police stations the probable details of James Blake's clothes and appearance.

"That's just in case," he explained to us. "It doesn't do to take the slightest risk at this stage in the game. No news has come in from Walters. I wonder what the devil is happening? I'm getting jumpy. . . . I think you are too, Mr. Jupp? And I don't blame you. . . . Three murders in as many days, almost. It's the damned unexpectedness of the thing that upsets me! That girl . . . you wouldn't have thought he'd have taken the risk, with the countryside full of police, and hot on his trail at that on account of the first two. He proved before that he was a cool worker, but last night's effort—it's incredible! Who could have foreseen it?"

He was talking to relieve his own anxiety. The case had overgrown itself, as it were, and while it lay in his hands like dough in a trough that was too small for it, had risen and spilt in spite of his efforts to hold it in. His responsibility was considerable, and I could imagine that he saw the case being taken from him by some big man from Scotland Yard. Subconsciously he was assuring George Jupp, who occupied a peculiar and privileged position in the police world, that he had done all that a police inspector could have done under the circumstances. The unfortunate fact that the criminal had slipped through his fingers even as they had been about to close upon him was just a piece of sheer bad luck. But in the meantime he *had* escaped, and unless Walters succeeded in following him, it might be several days, perhaps weeks— for the young man had shown himself to be singularly cun- ning—before he was finally caught, and between this moment and that the Inspector reasonably envisioned a period of criticism and recrimination.

Walters' disappearance had upset him: I think he saw cause in it not only for perplexity, but also for actual alarm. He could not forget that the detective had had to deal with a particularly desperate man, who, having killed the girl he loved to close her mouth, and murdered two other people within the week, was scarcely likely to hesitate before removing someone whom he rightly considered to stand between him and freedom. In short, Walters might have met with foul play, and that was a possibility Inspector English could not ignore, however reluctant he was to believe it.

Nothing more could be done at the moment beyond extending the scope of the search, and discussion could not produce anything. Jupp might have been ready to argue with the Inspector about his conclusions, but the Inspector was not in the best of moods to be told that he was altogether wrong —a mood which was not improved by the delivery of the Professor's morning newspapers.

It was many years since a war millionaire and a titled, high-brow, slightly scandalous lady had been murdered on successive days in the same neighbourhood—if indeed, it had ever happened. The journalists and the crime-reporters had let themselves go on the subject of Eastblyth's isolated eeriness. Brooker's Mill was presented with the adjective "haunted," and the police were said to be "powerless," although an arrest was "imminent." Column upon column of it.

The Inspector growled, pretended that it was a bad policy to allow newspapers to publish photographs, however unflattering, of police inspectors, and remarked that unless he speedily placed some kind of check at the junction of the main road and the road across the moor, the countryside would be one large car park before the afternoon. Suffolk, to say nothing of Norfolk, Essex and Cambridgeshire, would arrive in motor-cars and charabancs to gape at the scenes of the murders and assist in the investigation. By the evening the Londoners would begin to turn up.

"If only we could be left alone!" he went on, and added that the whole shoot would blow up when the third murder reached the public. I've got to have Blake under lock and key by that time!" he added savagely.

The demand, prayer, whatever it was, was fulfilled.

It happened in this way.

At about half-past ten, when we were gathered on the big lawn and about to reorganise the search-party into a more cohesive systematic body, two figures were seen slowly approaching the lower gate. They came on the dyke wall by which the foreshore and beach could be reached without descent to the lower-lying marshland.

Carstairs drew our attention to them, and pointed out that there was something "queer" about one of them. This queerness became in due course more definitely perceptible, and by the time the individual arrived at the gate and opened it, we realised what was the matter with him: he was covered from head to foot in heavy black swamp-mud, so that his clothes clung to him and the slanting morning sun shone and glittered on the greasy moisture with which he dripped. I saw that the other man, who did not appear to share the plight of the first, was a sheep-farmer called Josh Denny. His round, squat person was unmistakable—his mutton and lamb are excellent because his animals are marsh fed. He carried his usual long stick, and stumped along behind his companion.

Suddenly the Inspector uttered an exclamation.

"My God! That's *Walters*!" He set off toward the gate, and we realised that he had recognised the man in the mud suit as his missing detective. Jupp and I hurried after him.

"For Heaven's sake, sir," Walters greeted his chief, "tell this fool I'm not the murderer!"

"I caught un in my field," said Josh Denny firmly.

"Field! It was a forty-yard swamp! I was up to my neck in it, and if he hadn't heard my shouts I'd be in it yet."

"If he ain't the man whut's killed Mr. Page and the lady, I'd like to know who he is," continued Josh Denny suspiciously. "I ain't seed him afore, and he doan't belong to this parts—if he did, he'd have knowed better nor than get hisself bogged up in the Devil's Pool."

"He's a policeman," said the Inspector shortly. "Now, Walters, what does it all mean? Where's Blake?"

We left Josh Denny, a disappointed man, at the gate, and gathered round the detective. He sneezed, and said:

"I don't know where he is. He got away."

"Damn! How?"

"I saw a light go on in his room at three thirty-five a.m. I got up close to the back of the workshop, and after a few minutes the light went out. I heard him coming down the ladder, and saw him leave by the courtyard door. He was wearing a soft hat and a storm-proof; he was quite clear in the moonlight—the moon was in and out of the clouds most of the night."

"Was he carrying anything?"

"Not that I could see—he had his hands in his pockets."

"Go on. You followed him, of course."

"Yes, sir. He went down this grass path to the gate, and went through it on to the marshes. I came after him, keeping him within sight all the time, but not near enough for him to see me. But he knew I was somewhere about and following him, for he looked back several times, and once, when he was about a hundred yards along that dyke there, he turned right round and stood waiting for me to catch up with him. I was beneath the dyke, on the dark side, close to it—there wasn't much room between the slope and the ditch—and it's a six-foot ditch full of weeds and water. I was afraid I'd fall in any moment——"

"Get on! Get on!" muttered the Inspector impatiently.

"Yes, sir. Well, I stopped when he stopped, and after a moment he called out something about his going for a walk, and there being no point in my sneaking after him." He paused to wipe a smear of mud from his chin with a hand which was muddier. He sneezed again, and went on:

"Of course I wasn't going to take any notice of that sort of thing, and when he started off again I kept after him. It certainly looked as though he was only going for a walk, because down there there's only marsh and beach and sea—mud, stones and water. After about a mile, going Inderswick way, he left the dyke and moved slightly inland across the marsh. It was about four by then, and although the sky over the sea was a bit paler than it had been, the moon was about gone, and things seemed a lot darker. I had to decrease the distance between him and me to keep him in sight. He was going fairly quickly too. I don't know whether it was the darkness, the hurry, or a deliberate trap, but quite suddenly I found myself up to the calves in mud. I could see him in front, and I thought if he had crossed the bad bit I could. So I went on—and sank deeper. There's a path of firm ground across that swamp, it seems, but I didn't find it until the sheep man showed it to me half an hour ago. The surface all looks much alike. I got properly stuck—the more I moved the deeper I went. It put the wind up me. I saw the only thing to do was to wait until he came back, but he didn't, and it wasn't until——"

"Blake went on?"

"Yes, sir. When I realised I was really in——"

"Which way did he go?"

The detective sneezed again.

"I couldn't say for certain, sir, but since he didn't come back by the way he went, I think he must have struck inland to a road or lane. He knows those marshes all right. There's another thing, sir. Miss Skinner went off in the car about eleven, and she hadn't returned when I left at half-past three."

"Miss Skinner stayed at the Manor House last night, and was shot dead at her open window between three and four in the morning," the Inspector told him.

Walters started.

"He could have got round that way!" he muttered. "So *that* was why he bogged me, was it?"

"It looks like it. I asked you a moment ago if he was carrying anything. You're absolutely sure of that?"

Walters nodded.

"Unless, sir, it was under his rain-coat."

"That occurred to me. A ·22 rifle isn't very long, and it wouldn't show carried that way, particularly at night."

"The silencer would add seven or eight inches to its length," put in Jupp.

"Not if it was the screw-on type and could be stowed in one of his pockets," said the Inspector. "Grice"—he turned to the sergeant—"get on to the railway people at Saxmundham,

Darsham and Halesworth—also the A.A. and R.A.C. huts on the main road. Advise the police-stations that Walters has turned up and that James Blake is definitely loose somewhere. But before anything else ask the operator for a trunk call to Scotland Yard—priority. I'll talk to the Assistant-Commissioner and ask for a general circulation of the description. Blake may have got some distance. Walters, get a bath and some dry clothes. See the butler—he'll fix you up, I daresay."

Thus the wheels for a nation-wide search for James Blake were set in motion. While the Inspector spoke to Scotland Yard, Jupp and I were left to our own devices. I asked what chance he thought Blake had of getting away completely, and the little man was dubious of it.

"In these days it's very difficult to hide oneself for any length of time. Even if one gets abroad, the international police system is not an easy affair to circumvent. Blake might keep out of the way for months, or they might catch him this evening—assuming, of course, that he has really run away."

"Don't you think he has?" Once again he had startled me.

"I can't help feeling that he may have been simply telling the truth when he told Walters that he was only going for a walk. After all, what real evidence is there that he has bolted, except that he got up at three o'clock in the morning, told someone he was going for a walk, and is half an hour late for breakfast in that he hasn't shown up yet? Because a fool of a policeman lost himself in a mud-hole on a dark night trying to follow him doesn't necessarily mean that he was flying from justice. I can conceive James Blake turning round and pulling Walters out of that swamp if Walters had hollered for help like a sensible man."

"So can I," I said. "But granting that the swamp episode was a deliberate effort on Blake's part to get rid of him, he may still have been in the process of bolting. I tell you what I think. Last night, when I rang up this place and told them Anita was staying the night with us, Blake was considerably upset to hear it. He became abrupt with me, and more or less rang off. Anita was in the room while I was telephoning, and laughed when she realised what he was angry about. She had apparently told him she intended to marry me sooner or later——"

"Um?" said Jupp.

"She was one of those people who have to have a romantic ambition of some kind, preferably a new one for every day in the week," I explained.

"I see."

"Blake has been in love with her for some time: he was fed up, and saw in her wish to stay the night at the Manor not a way of avoiding her father in his state of irritation with her, but a method of encouraging whatever emotional feeling I might have for her. As I see it he went to bed after a tiring evening's work with Skinner, and could not sleep. He realised how useless it was to hope for anything where Anita was concerned; if you like, she had fallen from the pedestal on which he had placed her, and he could not put her back on it. He gave up all attempt at sleep and decided to clear out of the whole thing, felt he could not bear to see Anita again— imagined, perhaps, that her affair with me was in the active process of fulfilment: it wouldn't be an unreasonable suspicion in his lonely, desperate mood. He got up, dressed, and went out. He didn't wait to collect clothes——"

"Which suggests, surely, that he felt he needed a good long tramp by himself to clear his brain—to get things straightened out. A man about to run away takes his tooth-brush and safety razor, at least. Blake took neither. Nothing is missing from his room except a grey flannel suit, a rain-coat and a hat. He carried no bag. If you tell the Inspector, by the way, that Blake was jealous of you—and I think it's your duty to tell him—you'll satisfy him even further that he is the murderer. That is another motive for his killing the girl, and above all a motive for the attempt on you that night of the dinner-party. In fact, English will say that if it hadn't been for the quickness with which he decided to suspect Blake, you might well have been shot along with the others. Arden, you *will* have to tell him, I'm afraid, however convinced of Blake's innocence your liking for him has made you."

I was silent. I saw as clearly as did Jupp that such evidence might well prove to be the deciding factor in the case for the Crown which would condemn James Blake, and I did not like the thought of it at all. I got back to the original theme of our discussion.

"You think, then, that he's just off for a walk to clear his head?"

Jupp considered for a moment, and at length said:

"This jealousy business makes everything uncertain. I'm not sure but what I shan't have to begin again very nearly from the beginning. He may have bolted; he may even have had a ·22 under his coat, led Walters into the mud on purpose, made for the Manor House, and shot the girl about four o'clock—in fact, done everything the Inspector says he must have done. What time did Greene and Roberts change over? Two-hour watches beginning at eight p.m. Which means they *did* change over at four."

He drifted off into thought, and I walked by myself down the flagged path which fringed the southern wall of the house. I must confess I did not see then, any more than I do now, what vital difference Blake's jealousy could have made. He was jealous of me in a very general way; he had probably been equally jealous of the several men in whom Anita had from time to time taken a more than casual interest during the last two years.

I still denied that they would make a murderer out of him, however many motives they produced, however long the chain of circumstantial evidence with which they tied him to the crimes. He had not committed them; they could not prove he had. I began to hope fervently that Jupp was wrong and the Inspector right about his disappearance; I hoped that he had escaped and would never be seen again. I had no fear for him, once he had eluded them, for he possessed youth and brains. He would survive; he would forget Anita, and the trouble and heartburning she had brought him.

The Inspector came out into the garden after his telephone conversation with the Assistant-Commissioner, and Sergeant Grice took his place at the telephone in order to instruct the local police-stations in the new situation.

"Within ten minutes," English assured me, "every policeman in Great Britain will be on the look-out for him; the ports will be watched; and he'll have very little chance of getting free."

He seemed rather more cheerful than he had been before he telephoned, and I guessed that the Assistant-Commissioner had been recompensed for the third murder by the news that the murderer, if temporarily mislaid, was known and within reasonable likelihood of capture.

By this time I had decided to wait a little while before I added to the weight of evidence against the young man, realising that there need be no hurry to placate Jupp's social conscience. If necessary I would wait until Jupp himself forced me to speak, and I reflected that I had at least told him, and he could do what he liked about it.

He joined us, and the Inspector began to outline his procedure at the inquest that afternoon. He proposed to give all the evidence against Blake he could collect at such short notice—from now until three o'clock he would be in consultation with the Crown solicitor—and ask for an adjournment until the conclusion of the criminal proceedings. He had decided to lump all three murders together, and demonstrate their obvious similarity.

"Rushing things a bit, won't it be?" asked Jupp.

"A little, perhaps, but it will show everybody we have got the thing well in hand. It was the Assistant-Commissioner's idea."

"I can't help thinking about Mendholz," I put in. "Perhaps I'm prejudiced, having had something to do with the man all those years ago. Suppose your Norwich police missed something, somewhere. Norwich is only thirty-odd miles from here. He's got a 'leedle' motor-car."

"Suppose you suggest a motive," said the Inspector rather shortly. "And anyhow, if the Norwich people did miss something as you put it, there was one of my men outside

Mendholz' door at The Knife and Whistle all night, and the room is on the top floor, where he couldn't get out of any window. If he'd wandered out, he'd have been stopped. If he wandered out and wasn't stopped for some reason, it would have been reported to me hours ago. Mendholz is out of this. Has never been in it. It was odd his showing up—a bit of a coincidence—but that's all. He's out of it, Mr. Arden."

I sighed. I could not see what hope Blake had.

Grice appeared.

"I beg your pardon, sir, for interruptin', but Southwold's on the phone now. They've got Blake——"

"Thank God!" said the Inspector. "Where did they pick him up?"

"They didn't, sir. He walked in and said he had an appointment with you."

"At half-past eleven," remarked Jupp, and glanced at his watch. "He's punctual, anyway. That statement you wanted, Inspector, if you remember."

But the Inspector was too firmly in the grip of relief and satisfaction to realise the significance of this anti-climax.

"Tell them to put him in a cell," he said. "Arrest him as a suspected person, and tell 'em I'm coming over at once! Then get me Scotland Yard again. The chase is finished before it's begun. Statement, Mr. Jupp! He's given himself up! I shall have his complete confession before lunch."

But the Inspector had nothing of the kind before lunch, or indeed after. He arrived at the police-station to find James Blake in a fury at having been arrested. When the Inspector told him that he had committed his third murder during the night, he laughed in his face. When he learnt that it was Anita Skinner he was supposed to have killed he fainted; he came to and tried to break the Inspector's head with an ink-pot, and ended up in the cell again without having made any statement at all beyond a stark, categorical denial of his guilt and a short, trenchant speech of defiance. He told the Inspector to go to hell, and hang him if it would make him any happier, but that he would certainly be hanging the wrong man. With which he turned his back on the policemen and assumed an air of studied boredom.

At just that moment, about half-past twelve, Robina, the Reverend Lionel Lake's pretty housemaid, who was cleaning silver in the pantry of the Vicarage, heard a sound which she afterwards described as being "like as if you smacked the wall with your hand." It came from the back of the house somewhere, perhaps the lane which ran along the bottom of the garden behind the privet hedge. Almost simultaneously she heard a heavy thud in the master's study, followed by a silence which vaguely disturbed her. After about a minute she left her silver and went to the study. The door was closed; she knew the Vicar was inside, because he always was about that time. She knocked twice, received no answer, and opening the door saw the Vicar leaning far forward in his desk chair with his head lying on the blotting pad in front of him.

He was quite still, his eyes were closed, and on the white blotting-paper a round, bright red patch slowly increased in size.

CHAPTER XII

THE EFFECT of this, the fourth of the Eastblyth murders, was far greater in every way than was that of any of the preceding ones, and for the simple reason that it followed in all its respects the characteristics of the others, save in the one significant detail that it happened *after* the arrest of the man presumed by the Inspector to be guilty of the first three. Furthermore, it happened within half an hour of the police patrols being withdrawn from the neighbourhood, and at a time when the countryside was breathing more easily, reassured by the comforting news that the guilty man was in prison.

Nothing could have been more unfortunate from the Inspector's point of view than the accident of unkindly fate which caused a newspaper man, Alison Crew, the crime expert of the *Morning News* and *Evening Globe,* to walk past the Vicarage at the precise moment that Robina rushed screaming into the front garden. She saw Mr. Crew, and throwing herself through the gate, flung her arms round his neck, and told him, between hysterical cries, that the Vicar was lying dead at his desk "in there." This again was a circumstance which helped to arouse the subsequent furore.

Alison Crew at that particular moment was on his way back to lunch at The Knife and Whistle, having sent off a telegram in which he announced to his editor the arrest of the Eastblyth murderer and his intention of staying on for the inquest that afternoon. It had not been a very satisfactory case from his point of view, since Inspector English had with some success kept all the reporters at bay; whenever he had been persuaded to tell them something, he had effectively prevented anything in the nature of a scoop for anybody by gathering all the representatives together before opening his mouth. "Gentlemen," he said, "I always make a point of being fair with the Press."

But Alison Crew was an opportunist, and although the murderer had been caught, he still hoped cheerfully that some crumb of exclusive knowledge might fall his way.

It did not take him much more than a second and a half to realise that one had fallen with Robina, and brought a loaf. He hurried the maid back into the Vicarage in spite of her protests that they would all be murdered, shut the front door, and proceeded to acquire one of the greatest scoops of his career. Robina, at first incoherent, could tell him nothing, but after a few minutes she recalled the "funny noise" she had heard somewhere "out at the back." He diagnosed it as a silenced report of the weapon which had killed Mr. Lake, and he dashed into the small garden behind the house. There was nobody in it, and he penetrated the lane beyond by means of the lych gate. This lane, running between the Vicar's privet hedge on one side and a high bramble and hawthorn hedge on the other, marks for half a mile the southern boundary of the Manor House estate. It is sometimes called Sandy

Lane by the villagers, because of its surface, which is very loose. Alison Crew saw that it had been deeply rutted by cart-wheels, and that apparently every pair of feet which had walked along it for the last five years had left a track. There seemed to be hundreds of them, and he realised at once the futility of trying to determine which had been made by the murderer. The lane, as far as he could see in both directions, about seventy yards, was quite empty. This did not surprise him particularly, since it was obvious that the murderer had had at least seven minutes in which to get away. Mr. Crew was in a quandary. He felt certain that if he ran fast in the correct direction he stood a chance of catching a glimpse of the person who had shot the Vicar, but he was quite unable to decide whether to go to the right or left. A better knowledge of local topography might have sent him to the left, because the other way the lane ended abruptly after a hundred yards at the Corner Farm, and Mrs. Rosalba's new cottage. To the left lay the road across the moor, a more likely route of escape. Alison Crew almost wished, in spite of his reluctance to share his good fortune with anyone, that he had someone with him who might follow simultaneously the alternative direction. As it was he spent several moments in a state of indecision, and then tried to determine the place where the murderer had stood. He found four or five small holes in the privet hedge of a convenient size and height to admit a rifle aimed at the study window, but the soft nature of the ground and its multitude of blurred footmarks made it impossible to tell which the murderer had used. He returned to the house, and occupied himself for the next ten minutes in conducting what he termed "an investigation." He found eight packets of love-letters addressed to the Vicar and a diary which further enlightened him as to Mr. Lake's amorous interludes—a very indiscreet diary indeed, which Alison Crew decided could have no bearing on the case from the police point of view, but which, judiciously sub-edited, might prove enthralling matter for the readers of the *Morning News*. He put it in his pocket.

By this time Robina had sufficiently overcome her hatred of Mrs. Granville, the cook-housekeeper, to go into the kitchen and break the news. Mrs. Granville was deaf, and she had continued to prepare the Vicar's luncheon without hearing anything of what had been happening in the other side of the house.

While the two women enjoyed a mutual attack of hysteria and came to the conclusion that the police must be summoned, Alison Crew hurried up to the post-office at the end of the road, where, in the telephone box behind the drapery counter, he spoke for ten minutes to the Fleet Street offices of the *Morning News* and *Evening Globe*. He then called up the police-station, and informed Inspector English of the murder. He heard the horrified perplexity in the Inspector's voice, and replied but vaguely to his injunction that on no account was anybody to be told what had happened.

"No newspaper man!" said English. "Wait for me at the Vicarage! I shall want your evidence! Who is speaking, by the way?"

"My name's Crew."

"All right. Mind what I say—tell nobody——"

Alison Crew, having told the world before he had told the Inspector (if only by a minute or so), hung up the receiver, and went back to the Vicarage to await, with that certain feeling of something accomplished, something done, the arrival of the police.

He was interested to see what the Inspector would say about James Blake's arrest in the light of this further extension of the crime, for he was enough of an expert himself to realise that the circumstances and manner of the Vicar's death, following accurately the precedent of the other three, suggested that the same hand was responsible.

It was not until after lunch that I heard the details of the discovery of the fourth murder; Jupp, who had been at the police-station when Alison Crew rang up the Inspector, told me about it. He accompanied English to the Vicarage, missing his lunch in order to do so, and reaching the Manor House when the meal was over.

But before that I had a surprise. About fifteen minutes to one I entered my drawing-room by the french windows from the garden, now free of patrolling constables, and came face to face with no less a person than Professor Skinner! He was standing with his back to the fireplace, his hands clasped behind his lean back, and his expression set and hard-mouthed; you could not tell what he was feeling.

"Hullo!" I exclaimed. "I thought you were in London!"

"No. I went to Ipswich to see Gardner, my—er—local solicitor." He paused, and added unemotionally: "Carstairs told me about Anita when I got home a short time ago."

He jerked his head, indicating the room above us, where the girl's body lay.

"That damned policeman has locked the door, your butler tells me."

"Yes. Er—I——"

"Don't for God's sake say how grieved you are about her. You've got over the shock by now—so have I—and that's all there is to it. You're not grieved. Neither am I. Call me hard, if you like. Daresay I am. Only thing to be in this world. As hard as you damned well can be. She was my own flesh and blood—biologically, eh? Nothing more. She hated me. Always did. I didn't hate her, but I don't think I ever liked her. She was exactly the same as her mother—selfish, cowardly, sensation-seeking. She reminded me of Phillida to an extent that would have been ludicrous if it hadn't been so blasted uncomfortable. But the girl's dead. The chap with the rifle has got her too. Carstairs says it was Jimmy Blake—that he's been arrested, and so on. Well, if it was, he had reason, I expect. It occurred to me, walking over here just now, that he may have been in love with her and she made a game of him. Played him up, you know. Jimmy has a funny temper."

"He didn't kill her," I said.

"Jupp doesn't think so?"

"He doesn't. In fact, he went over to Southwold half an

hour ago to see him—to cheer him up. The trouble is, though, that appearances are extraordinary against him. He hasn't an alibi for a single night; and last night he got up at half-past three and went off somewhere, and wasn't seen again, as far as anybody knows up to the present, until half-past eleven, when he walked into the police-station."

"What the devil did he do that for?"

"The Inspector asked him to yesterday, if you remember—to make a statement."

The Professor nodded.

"Well, I saw Gardner this morning—he's a good man. He agreed that I ought to try and get Critchley-Jenkins interested."

"Who is Critchley-Jenkins, exactly?"

"He's that criminal lawyer who did so well with the Cuffley blackmail case."

"I remember."

"I wanted to have Gardner's opinion, you see," he explained —rather lamely, I thought.

I invited him to stay to lunch, and he accepted gratefully. His self-sufficiency and detachment from the tragedy which had come upon him were amazing, and although I knew him to be utterly lacking in the normal human emotions of parenthood, I found it difficult to believe that he was not concealing a greater grief than appeared in his voice and bearing.

We did not wait lunch for Jupp, since it had been agreed that while the excitement was still at its height meal-times should be regarded as matters of personal convenience rather than formal, clock-governed functions, and the Professor attacked the meal with the normal, healthy appetite of an untroubled man. He even talked casually of Anita's tiresome methods of putting brightness into life, and spoke of them as finished and done with; there was nothing of the sentimental present tense phrasing of it, as though she were still alive.

Presently he began to discuss, or rather deliver a scientific monologue on the subject of his new field-gun, and I gathered that it was almost out of the experimental stage. When he had got it ready for the War Office tests, he assured me people would sit up and think twice about the theory that future wars would be affairs of air raids, gas and heavy, long-range artillery of the Big Bertha category. He finished up by adding:

"Young Blake is no murderer. He attacks me sometimes about the wickedness of improving weapons of war. I think he's what one would call a humanitarian at heart. He doesn't like to think of people being killed."

I said nothing, although I very much agreed with Blake. As long as there are Professor Skinners in the world the peace-makers will never succeed in outlawing war; invent an engine of destruction, and you invent a dozen, for you will set rivals at work. To argue with them, to point out their folly, is a certain waste of time and breath, and I had long ago discovered the Professor to be particularly impatient of such evangelistic efforts. So I held my tongue, and merely said that I also could not imagine Blake to be capable of murder.

"Jupp," remarked the Professor, "won't let him hang. He'll find the right man for them."

"He has impressed you, then?"

"Yes, he struck me as being the quiet, observant type with a faculty for thinking straight. When you and I *feel* that Jimmy couldn't have committed these foul crimes, he probably *knows* he didn't, and, if he liked, could explain with fact and evidence how he came to know."

I was rather astonished at this tribute to a man whom, after all, he had not seen more than once, and then but for a few minutes under circumstances of no great comfort from the point of view of forming a judgment.

"So you think he may be on the right track?"

"He isn't the man to visit Jimmy just to cheer him up; he went for information, and he'll get it."

Lunch came to an end. The inquests on Page and Lady Codrington were to be held simultaneously at three o'clock at the Towers, and I proposed to attend. I concluded that Jupp, since he had neither put in an appearance nor sent a message, would not show up until then, but within five minutes of the Professor's departure he arrived with Inspector English and Sergeant Grice. They came straight from the Vicarage with the news of the Vicar's death.

"My God!" I cried, "that's the fourth. And Blake *can't* have done this one——"

The Inspector was in a thoroughly uncomfortable state of mind. His mouth was set in a grim line, and at the name of Blake he frowned and tugged at his small moustache.

"The Vicar was killed while I was questioning that young man in the charge-room of the police-station. I've arrested him, and charged him with the murder of Anita Skinner, further charges impending. I'd have fixed the other killings on him, too—and now *this* has happened! My God, Mr. Arden! It looks as though that chap who found the Vicar's body may be right. There's nothing to connect this murder with the others, and there's no sense in it. It's the work of a madman!"

"A madman?" I said.

Jupp told me then how Alison Crew had stumbled upon the fourth murder, and of Alison Crew's suggestion that the whole business from the beginning had been the work of a maniac, who had emerged from his hiding-place in some wood or hole on the moor to let loose his rifle bullets at inoffensive, unsuspecting residents.

"The only trouble about that, of course," added Jupp, "is the fact that the maniac patiently waited for the police patrols to be withdrawn before attempting to kill Mr. Lake. Intelligent maniac. And well-informed."

"Unless he's hiding close about here," said the Inspector. "Anyway, I'm not going to let the possibility go untried. I'll comb this countryside, if I have to muster the whole East Suffolk police force."

He was reaching an almost desperate state of mind, and probably realised that it was now inevitable that Scotland Yard would have to be consulted with a view to assistance. Looking at the affair impartially, four murders had been committed within four days, and he had done nothing toward solving the mystery save in as far as he had arrested a man

146

who now seemed unlikely to be guilty. Yet Jupp, who by that time may or may not have had an inkling as to the truth, and was a far more gifted investigator than the Inspector, could not have blamed him in any respect save perhaps in the blind determination with which he had set out to prove that James Blake was the murderer. He might have employed the time he had wasted over him in some other and more profitable direction, but it was difficult to see where this lay. Jupp himself, in fact, given the Inspector's powers, could have done little more; he could neither have prevented a single murder nor arrested the guilty man. Jupp had suspicions, but no evidence—not a shred of evidence, and as far as he could see, even at that late hour, no means of obtaining any. He was sorry for the Inspector, and I believe he would have extended him a helping hand at that moment if he could have done without straining the policeman's credulity to breaking point at a time when his thoughts and suspicions were already chaotic. I also felt keenly for the Inspector; he had been up against a far more difficult state of affairs than he had realised, and it was only now, when so much damage had been done, that he was beginning to grasp the fact. He was like an over-confident swimmer who discovers himself to be out of his depth, and that he is further from the shore than he thought.

"It doesn't make sense . . ." he said. "I'm damned if it makes sense!"

"I wish we had tried to get in touch with the Professor this morning," remarked Jupp irrelevantly.

I sprang the surprise.

"He's home again," I said, and told them how the Professor had gone no further than Ipswich, and on returning to "Windy Arbour" had heard about his daughter's death.

"You say he's been here lunching with you?" cried the Inspector in astonishment. "What was he doing over here, and what time did he come?"

"Anita's body is still upstairs."

"Yes. That's a good enough reason. But what time did he come? What time did he get back from Ipswich?"

He was as eager on this new trail as he had been on Blake's an hour or so ago—a drowning man snatching at straws.

"He said he had come straight over," I replied, "and he arrived here some time between twelve fifteen and a quarter to one."

"Can't you narrow it down closer than that?"

"By asking Jeames, I daresay. You see, I was in the garden before lunch, and came into the drawing-room to find him waiting there for me. That was at quarter to one."

"Excuse me," said the Inspector, and rang the bell. Jeames came, and without hesitation fixed the time at which Professor Skinner had come through the front door at twelve thirty-nine.

The Inspector almost leapt at him.

"How do you know—to a minute like that?" he demanded.

Jeames remained as unaffected as ever—an imperturbable man.

"I looked at the clock, sir," he said.

"What made you look at the clock?"

Jeames raised his distinguished eyebrows.

"I really cannot say, sir, unless perhaps I wondered how Professor Skinner had succeeded in getting to London and back in four and a half hours. I concluded, if I may make so bold, sir, that Professor Skinner had not gone to London, and that my informant was incorrect in stating that he had."

"Your informant?" I said sharply.

"Mr. Carstairs, of 'Windy Arbour,'" replied Jeames.

"Why should he tell you that his master had gone to town?"

"I beg your pardon, sir, but I asked him."

"Asked him if the Professor had gone to town?" said Jupp.

"No, sir. I merely asked, over the telephone, where Professor Skinner might be."

We stared at him, and I suppose—I cannot say more than "suppose," for if I live to be a hundred (and Jeames to be a hundred and thirty) I shall never discover how or why he does such a lot of things—I suppose, then, he felt at this period that he ought to explain his interest in one of his social superiors, the interest of a butler in a great and notable scientist. He said, exploding a small bomb-shell:

"The moment I had time to think this morning, after Mrs. Jeames had quietened down after her very unpleasant experience, I remembered something I had heard the Professor say to Miss Skinner. I was present in the hall when it was said, sir." He turned to me. "That was the occasion of the dinner-party on the tenth, sir. The Professor said: 'Anita, my girl, I sometimes think that shooting would be too swift a death for you.'"

There was a moment's silence.

"A man doesn't say a thing like that seriously," I observed. "I think Jeames over-estimated the significance of the remark."

Jeames slightly inclined his head.

"Three days later Miss Skinner was found shot, sir," he said. The Inspector made an impatient gesture.

"How was the remark made? In anger? In a joking way?"

"The Professor, sir, seemed rather put out about something that had happened."

"What was it?"

"That, sir, I'm afraid I do not know," replied Jeames reluctantly.

"When you rang up Carstairs," said Jupp, "did you tell him that Miss Skinner had been killed?"

"Certainly not, sir. To do that would have interfered with the proper course of Inspector English's investigations. It was not my place to inform Mr. Carstairs of Miss Anita's lamentable death."

We gathered from the tone of his last four words that he had always believed that she would come to what is called a bad end. Jeames is nothing if he is not mid-Victorian; the Anita Skinners of this modern world must be considerably more than he can stomach.

"Thank you, Mr. Jeames," said the Inspector, and the worthy man withdrew with an air which suggested that the Inspector would be a fool if he did not turn his attention to the Professor's activities during the last few days.

I do not know whether Jeames had heard of the Vicar's murder at that early moment, but I wondered how he, or indeed anyone else, could hope reasonably to lay it at the Professor's door. But in the course of the next half-hour it became clearly apparent that that was what would be attempted. Jupp was directly responsible, even if the Inspector was by then more than ready to accept any encouragement he could get toward forming a fresh theory.

Jupp let loose at the Inspector his idea about "The Silent Skinner" and the possibility that the shot fired at me during the dinner-party had come from inside the room, and not from the wood on the other side of the lawn. To it he added a new scrap of supporting evidence.

"If you remember, the bullet Arden found on the floor after it had struck the panelling was a soft lead one—not nickel-plated. Why? Suppose that the pistol could only take lead? It is unnecessary to point out the obvious advantage of the nickel-plated type, with its greater penetrating power and its longer effective range such as were used for the actual murders. In fact, I do not see why we should not consider that Arden owed his life to the well-known self-conceit of the creative mind. Only Professor Skinner could have had such faith in 'The Silent Skinner' as to entrust to it a task so important as murder."

The policeman did not display an immediate enthusiasm for this pistol business, but I saw that once he had overcome a pique and a little professional jealousy he would be hot on the trail of "The Silent Skinner."

"Motive?" he asked. "Where's the motive?"

"Assuming that multiple murderers are more usually insane than sane," said Jupp, "I have come to the conclusion, as this case has become more and more involved, that it merely complicates it further to attach too much significance to the question of motive. A lack of discernible motive should not deter us from seeking evidence in any direction. The Professor has spent a lifetime over-working; he was cursed by an unfortunate marriage and an unlovable daughter; indeed a daughter about whose morals the less said was usually the better. Recently the Government has shown a strong sympathy for international disarmament, and a reluctance, in its passion for economy, to spend money on an experimental field-gun. Reasons enough, surely, to upset a man's mental balance?"

"To the point of homicidal mania?" I asked.

"Certainly. The pathology is not inconsistent."

"But the Vicar? Unless Skinner was jealous of his association with Lady Codrington——"

"That's it!" said the Inspector. "He decided to kill them both! That's clear enough. But why did he try to kill Mr. Arden. And then there's the millionaire——"

Jupp spread out his hands.

"Ask Arden—he's one of the two."

"I can't think of a single reason," I said.

"No more can I," agreed the Inspector; "but if, as Mr. Jupp suggests, Professor Skinner is mad, why then I'll admit that it would be pretty well useless to look for motives all the way through."

Thus, with the Press opinion, voiced by Alison Crew, that somewhere in the neighbourhood a Nihilist lurked, firmly set upon exterminating the gentry of Eastblyth, and with Jupp apparently on the Professor's trail, we had two schools of thought, to both of which Inspector English subscribed. He shuffled off the inquests that afternoon in a very short time, being granted a fortnight's adjournment, after formal evidence of identification had been taken and the coroner had expressed his intention of holding the inquests on Miss Anita Skinner and the Rev. Lionel Lake at three o'clock on the morrow. He also took the opportunity of assuring the public that although the police had been called upon to solve one of the greatest mysteries of the century, and were faced with considerable difficulties, much had already been done, and the situation, grave as it might seem, was safely in hand.

Before the Inspector left to deal with these matters, to raise his forces and interrogate the Professor, I asked him what he proposed to do about James Blake, for according to the admirable law of this country he was not permitted to be kept in gaol for more than twenty-four hours without being brought before a magistrate.

"I have evidence enough to charge him with the murder of Miss Skinner," he said, "but in view of these developments I must hesitate to do that."

He did not, however, say how he proposed to keep hold of the young man until he had decided definitely that, in spite of all appearances to the contrary, he must be innocent. I saw his point; although Blake could not have killed the Vicar, there was nothing at present to prove that the person who had done so had not merely imitated the fashion of murder prevailing in our neighbourhood at the moment. Given the means, and the need, it would be quite a sensible method to employ. In other words, there might be two murderers.

I suggested this to Jupp, who characteristically, and not unreasonably, remarked that for that matter there might be four. But he didn't seriously think there was likely to be more than one.

" 'Just the one,' as Douglas Furber might say if you've ever played Bridge with him," he added mysteriously, and went off on his own somewhere.

I spent the afternoon writing the first half of this account of the Eastblyth murders, and found my study a quiet and fitting place in which to work. The day drew to its golden close, and I had Jeames bring me tea at about five o'clock.

"There are some policemen in the gardener's shed again, sir," he told me.

"The Inspector looks upon me as a likely victim."

He regarded me with troubled, faded eye.

"If anything happens to me," I said, "you and Mrs. Jeames will be provided for."

"Thank you, sir, thank you—but that was not what was in my mind. I do hope, sir, that you won't expose yourself to needless risk."

I assured him that I would take care of myself, and that

for the rest of the day I proposed to remain indoors at my desk.

I wrote on until six, when Jupp showed up again. I asked him where he had been, and he replied vaguely "round and about." He brought, however, a certain amount of news, of which the most significant he considered to be a discovery made by the Inspector at "Windy Arbour." Anticipating some kind of passive resistance, or at least an unwillingness to afford help, on the part of the Professor, he had armed himself with a search warrant, of which he had proceeded to make use in spite of the Professor's fury. But nobody, not even Critchley-Jenkins had he arrived in time, could have put the Inspector off. His insistence had been well rewarded: he had found a ·22 rifle which did not appear with the other four on the Firearms Certificate held by the Professor! James Blake had stated quite definitely in the original inquiry that the certificate was always kept up to date. This rifle was to be examined by an expert in order to determine whether it had been recently fired. Also there had come to light a specimen of "The Silent Skinner," but about this Jupp was inclined to be unenthusiastic. He did not think, although the Inspector had been eager to ignore the point, that it could have been the pistol used at the famous dinner-party. Its working parts were very rusty, and the trigger almost impossible to pull, so stiff had it become in the course of the idle years. The Inspector had tried the experiment of producing this weapon somewhat suddenly in the Professor's presence, but it had aroused no emotion in him save perplexity. He said: "I looked for one of those silly things the other day, and couldn't find one. Where did you find it?" He had been only casually interested in it, and if he guessed the direction of the Inspector's theory, he showed no sign of it. He was still fermenting inside with anger and outraged dignity. That anybody should suspect him, the great scientist, a man who had conferred inestimable benefit upon his country, smacked of lunacy, and although that lunacy might be obvious to the meanest intelligence, it was none the less aggravating to contend with. In effect, Professor Skinner had found the Inspector tiresome, and had told him so.

"The Inspector's pleased with himself," said Jupp, "and yet he's no nearer the truth than he was. The Professor's got a rotten alibi for the time Lake was shot. He says he came here this morning to see his daughter's body and talk to you. He walked because the news of her death had come as a shock to him, and he wanted a little time alone to adjust himself to it. The walk through the quiet woods appealed to him as a means of achieving this. He had arrived home by hired car from Darsham station at about eleven forty-five, and Carstairs had immediately broken the news to him; he had not even hung up his hat; he set off for the Manor at once. Jeames said that he reached this front door at twelve thirty-nine. During the three-quarters of an hour he took to cover the two and a half miles—by the footpath it's just about that —he says he saw no one and to the best of his knowledge was seen by no one. The Inspector cannot escape the fact that he could have made a slight detour and crossed the field along the south side of which runs Sandy Lane. English has found a gap in the hedge which gives quite an adequate view across the lane and the Vicarage garden to the study windows. He also found that the grass by that gap had been trodden down some time to-day. He discovered this as twilight came, and he has put a policeman there to guard it. In the morning he hopes to find more definite traces."

Jupp was sitting on the corner of my desk while he told me all this, and I wondered if it was my imagination or whether his eyes were indeed fixed on my face with an unusual intensity, as though he had at last made some progress in what must have been one of the really difficult cases of his career. I did not believe that he still held the Professor's theory, which, after all, he had produced originally as a kind of antidote to the Inspector's suspicion of James Blake, and not as a serious supposition. I asked a question.

"Did the Inspector put up any convincing theory as to how, when and where Skinner collected his rifle after leaving

Carstairs, and how, when and where he got rid of it after committing the crime and before arriving at this house in such good time?"

"No, but he has several. His best is his belief that after the murder of the girl the Professor hid his weapon somewhere in these grounds, in a hollow tree, or at all events near the footpath, where it would be comparatively easy for him to pick it up, shoot the Vicar and put it back before coming on here."

"Ingenious," I said. "But that suggests a considerable degree of foresight on Skinner's part."

"The Inspector is not frightened to suggest it, and I personally see no reason why he should be. I see nothing else but one long intricate but well-connected plan all the way from the beginning. A trifling arrangement like a hollow tree, for instance, is not out of the way—is not inconsistent with this view. Point to a single incident during the process of these murders, and show that it was unpremeditated."

I looked at him in silence for a moment, striving to read his mind. I was very much in the dark as to what he really thought, and I found it singularly disturbing. He remained, however, quite unconcerned on my account.

"Two things have caused English a lot of discomfort," he said after a pause. "One is the fact that Mr. Crew—he's the man who telephoned to the police-station when he had found the Vicar—is a newspaper man. Scotland Yard rang up an hour ago, wanting to know if the story in the *Evening Globe* is true. It was in print and on the streets by four-thirty! The Inspector's very sick about it. He was going to keep the affair absolutely quiet as long as possible—until the morning if he could—intending to get as much done as was humanly possible before writing an official report to-night for Scotland Yard's reading to-morrow. However, he has asked them for assistance. He had to, of course; what else could he do? He's shown he was on the wrong track by arresting Blake, and public opinion is something which even a policeman has to take notice of. Alison Crew's papers are going to shout about police inefficiency—four murders in four days, three of them under the Inspector's nose. Wisely, then, he has passed the buck, as the Americans say, and escaped the full weight of responsibility before it flattened him out altogether. He feels that he has missed the chance of his career, however, and I think he is right. He will have to wait a long time before a case as difficult and as sensational comes his way." He paused, and added: "I'm frightened of one thing——"

"—and that is?"

"That Scotland Yard may try to put me in charge. They've done it before, and in this affair they know I have been here since the beginning."

"Why should that frighten you?"

"Because I doubt if I could bring this case to a satisfactory conclusion."

"Why not?"

"There is an almost total lack of evidence," said Jupp gloomily.

"And by satisfactory conclusion you mean a conviction?"

"I mean a sentence of death."

The queer wolf-like intentness which I had noticed once before shone in his pale eyes for a moment, and I realised how passionately he loved his job.

"You know who the man is?" I asked, but he would not answer that. Either in pretence or in fact he had fallen into thought, and did not hear me. He left the study after a minute or two, and I went on writing. While I had the opportunity and the inclination I proposed to get as much done at the first sitting as I could manage.

In daylight from the study windows one can see across the lawn and woods to the southern boundary of the Manor House estate, and it was perhaps half an hour afterwards that I saw a light flickering along the hedge of Sandy Lane, opposite the Vicarage garden. The autumn evening had swallowed up the world, and I could not see who carried the lantern, but I guessed that it must be Jupp and the Inspector pursuing the evidence they needed so badly.

About seven o'clock, when I was beginning to feel the strain of several hours' writing, I went downstairs, and found Jupp asleep in an armchair in the lounge. I awoke him, and offered him sherry. He apologised for his sleepiness, and attributed it to his energetic day in the rich Eastblyth air. We dined alone together, and talked a certain amount during the meal. He inquired how my literary efforts were progressing, and I asked him a few questions that I might verify one or two technical details in the account. When I demanded to know how things were going, he showed a readiness to enlighten me. He had been with the Inspector the whole time, apparently, and had helped in the organisation of a big police and civilian force which was now at work combing the countryside immediately about the village. The police patrols were re-established in the gardens of the various houses and in the roads and lanes. Professor Skinner was being closely watched, but with discretion.

"He has been occupied in the workshops all the afternoon," Jupp said. "Blake, by the way, has asked to see him, and the Professor is going to visit him at the police-station some time to-night. That young man is in a more tractable mood, and has come to the conclusion that the affair is nearing its end. He has forgiven the Inspector for unjustly suspecting him, and says that now he has had time for reflection he sees that the Inspector could not have done anything else under the circumstances. He says that the shock of Anita Skinner's death temporarily upset his equilibrium, and that he lost his head when he suddenly found himself arrested and accused of her murder. The Inspector proposes to release him soon, probably to-morrow morning, not because his good behaviour has convinced him, but because the quality of the evidence against him is so slenderly circumstantial. English says quite reasonably that he can always pull him in again should he find stronger and more direct evidence. The fourth murder was done when he was under lock and key, and you can't get round the fact."

"What does Blake want to see the Professor about?" I asked.

Jupp shrugged his shoulders.

"He hasn't seen fit to tell us, but he wants to see him rather badly, and nobody is in any kind of position to refuse the request. Besides, it may lead somewhere—the interview."

We were silent for several minutes, until I observed, perhaps rather sombrely:

"Skinner and I are the only two left of the six who had dinner at this table on the night of the tenth."

"You are both being looked after," said Jupp. "The Inspector is very determined that nothing shall happen to either of you. He is quite sure that the Vicar would be alive still but for the unfortunate withdrawal of the police patrol. He is inclined to call that the greatest mistake of his career; he is unhappy about it. But he is equally certain that there will not be another murder, now that the police guards are organised again."

"Comforting," I said. "I am almost inclined to let Jeames open the curtains and let a little air into the room."

"I would not advise it, sir, if you will pardon me," said Jeames from the neighbourhood of the sideboard, and I bowed to his concern. Jupp continued to recount the details of his afternoon's investigations with the Inspector, but, for some reason I could not immediately determine, he said nothing of any visit by lantern light to the gap in the hedge of Sandy Lane. I wondered if I had been wrong in thinking it had been they, and decided that I had not. If, as Jupp had earlier told me, there was a constable on duty there he would never have permitted anybody else such near approach. I came to the conclusion, finally, that the detectives had found something, and proposed to keep silent about it. I began in no casual way to ask myself what it could have been. A wisp of wool on a twig where the rifle had been pushed through the hedge? A footmark, or some other definite clue? I hesitated to put a straight question to him about it, and contented myself with observing the occasional movement of expression on his difficult face. It told me nothing, of course.

"You saw Blake, I gather?" I remarked.

"Yes. You know, I shouldn't be surprised to discover later on that he has an inkling of the truth—or, at least, what he feels is the truth. Of course a man who has spent a day in a cell, and who is unaccustomed to cells, is likely to be in an unsettled state of mind, but Blake struck me, when I saw him an hour ago, to be suffering from what is termed 'suppressed excitement'—as though, in fact, he had an idea."

"It's about the idea, then, that he wants to see Skinner? It may be some theory of the murder he has evolved, but, on the other hand, he may be merely in the grip of a notion of how to get a half-ton shell another five miles. It's the sort of thing he would go on thinking about whether he was suspected of murder or not."

"Um," agreed Jupp, and finished his wine. He gazed at the empty glass without setting it on the table again, and changing the subject, asked:

"I suppose you have kept the fragments of the wine-glass the bullet smashed—the night you were shot at?"

I re-directed the question to Jeames by glancing across the room at him.

"I am afraid, sir, I threw them away."

"Pity!" Jupp murmured. "How many were there?"

"Two, sir."

"Only two?"

"The bulb and the stem; the base was not detached from the stem, sir."

"At the time," I said, "I decided that the bullet must have just touched the stem a little below my fingers."

"Did the wine make a lot of mess when you dropped it?"

"There was no wine in it. I had just drunk it."

"Mr. Arden," Jeames interposed with faint pride, "did not drop the bulb of the glass, but continued to hold it."

"Commendable *sang-froid*," remarked Jupp.

"Only the stem fell on to my napkin, on my knees," I said.

Jupp nodded, and twiddled the wine-glass in his hand.

"Was it anything like this one?"

"Of the same set, sir."

"Very thin stem," Jupp commented, and put it down at last. "Wouldn't present much obstacle to a bullet—if it happened to be passing that way."

"Exactly," I said. "And yet I've wondered once or twice since if it wasn't just enough to deflect it those few inches, and thus save my life."

"It's feasible," admitted Jupp, and did not speak again for the rest of dinner. I respected his mood, and after coffee established him in a comfortable chair in the study to think or read as he chose while I got on with my writing.

Before he went to his room for the night, however, he made one more remark which startled me. He said:

"Inspector English has put a dictaphone with a microphonic attachment below the peep-hole of Blake's cell door."

I looked at him.

"To record his conversation with Skinner?" I asked. He nodded, and said:

"We'll get the result to-morrow. Good-night."

"Good-night."

I returned to my manuscript, and did not go to bed until I had reached this point in the story. While I wrote I heard every now and again in the quiet night the steady tramp of a policeman's boots on the gravel path below the windows.

CHAPTER XIII

IMMEDIATELY after a nine o'clock breakfast the Inspector arrived with a square black suit-case and a telegram; the suit-case contained a dictaphone, and the telegram was a confirmation of the one received by Jupp half an hour previously. The Inspector was rueful, but glad that he was already on such good terms with Jupp.

"I didn't know you were attached to the C.I.D., Mr. Jupp."

"Sometimes they attach me," said Jupp. He smiled one of his rare, friendly smiles, and added: "But it can't be helped.

And with regard to any success we may have in this case it will be equally yours, Inspector, and when I write my report I shall make a point of telling the Commissioner so. You've had all the work to do, and I hope you will do a lot more. We'll run in double harness."

The Inspector's expression was grateful. He knew Jupp meant what he said; if the affair was satisfactorily concluded, he would not claim all the honour. Jupp had skilfully averted what easily might have been an uncomfortable situation.

English produced his patent dictaphone.

"In any case, I was going to ask you to listen to the record of the conversation between Blake and the Professor. It's interesting, and considering one or other may be guilty, he conceals the fact pretty well. Their conclusions are ridiculous, of course; they even discuss the possibility of Mr. Arden here being the murderer! It'll amuse you, Mr. Arden—young Blake deciding that if he could hit on an accomplice for you you would be the most likely murderer in the neighbourhood!"

I laughed.

"I suppose I needed an accomplice to shoot bits off that wine-glass."

Jupp looked gloomy.

"That's all he decided?"

"That's what the conversation led to. Both men were in queer moods."

"They must have been," I commented. "Did the Professor agree with Blake?"

"Not entirely. But you shall hear——"

The dictaphone was placed on the study table, and a wax cylinder set moving under the needle. A horn instead of the usual earphones amplified the sound, and eerily the voices of the two men who had talked together late last night in the cell broke the silence of the room. It was quite easy to distinguish the speakers, and I gathered from the fact that the Professor said rather abruptly: "He's a damned muddler, and I don't believe that the fellow Jupp is much better——!" that the machine had not been started simultaneously with the beginning of the conversation; and I wondered what their greeting had been like.

Blake apparently agreed with his employer that the detectives were not shining particularly. As nearly as I can recall it—and I think I am being fairly accurate, for I am writing it down within a few hours of hearing it—the conversation continued as follows:

Blake.—They can't go on saying I'm the murderer now the Vicar's been killed. Even English sees that. He's got to let me out.

Skinner.—So you didn't slaughter all those people?

Blake.—I assure you, sir, I did not. With one of them I was in love.

Skinner.—Anita.

(There was a moment's silence.)

Blake.—What's that scratching noise?

Skinner.—What scratching noise?

(Apparently caused by the dictaphone outside the cell. But they forgot about it, and if one or other or both of them realised what it was, they ignored it. After all, they felt they had nothing to fear from having their conversation recorded.)

Blake.—I've been thinking a good deal to-day, and I've tried to work the thing out in as detached a way as possible. You see, I'm not going to rest until the murderer of Anita is dead.

Skinner.—Melodramatic, my boy.

Blake.—If you like, sir. In fact, of course it is. If four murders in four days isn't melodramatic, I should like to know what is. Well, I've been thinking, and as far as I can see, you're the next on the list.

Skinner.—To be murdered?

Blake.—Yes. And to be suspected. Have you noticed how the moment a person has been suspected or considered to be implicated, he or she gets a bullet through the head? It's astonishing. If I'd been at that dinner-party, I'd consider myself a very likely victim from the moment I got out of here.

Skinner.—Sounds mad. In fact, everything about this terrible affair is mad. I mean, why should all these people get murdered simply because they went to the same dinner-party? What was peculiar about that dinner? Except the bullet coming in out of the garden and nearly hitting Arden——

Blake.—I didn't attend the dinner, so I can't say what was peculiar about it. But you did, sir, and that's why I wanted to see you to-night.

Skinner.—Oh! I thought you had decided to confess, and explain that you simply had to kill Anita after the disgusting way she treated you. I don't *know* how she treated you, but I can't believe it was too well.

Blake.—Anita was different from other women.

Skinner.—Yes, yes. But the subject is painful. So you want to know what was peculiar about the dinner at the Manor? I'm damned if I noticed anything. You mean, you want some connecting link, as it were, binding us all together in that it made our deaths either necessary or expedient to one particular person?

Blake.—Exactly.

Skinner.—Well, I can only repeat that I did not notice anything. It was just an ordinary dinner-party.

Blake.—Arden gave it.

Skinner.—What's peculiar in that?

Blake.—It becomes peculiar when you regard the fact that four of his five guests are already dead.

Skinner.—I can't see that. It's no more peculiar than the fact that four of those five all lived within five miles of one another. Within two, leaving me out. Arden has given that same party, with additions or subtractions, nearly every week for a couple of years.

Blake.—All right. Let's take the bullet. That was peculiar enough. Are you sure it came in through the window?

Skinner.—Of course it came in through the window. Where else can it have come from?

Blake.—Could Arden have fired it himself from a pistol of some kind? A silenced pistol?

Skinner.—Utterly impossible. He had both hands on the table when the bullet came, one of them holding his wine-glass. Utterly impossible! I can't see what you're driving at unless you're trying to suggest that Arden is the murderer. And that's ridiculous.

Blake (slowly).—If I could name an outside person who was his accomplice on that occasion I would suggest it very definitely indeed.

Skinner.—You're not thinking clearly. You can't forget that Anita was in love with him.

Blake.—I can't!

Skinner.—You don't murder a woman for being in love with you. Seldom if ever.

Blake.—No-o.

Skinner.—It's extremely improbable that this affair has all these deep subtleties in it. We shall find that there's some maniac lurking in the neighbourhood who has a grudge against society and who has found admirable opportunities for expressing it during the last few days. I am prepared to believe that he came upon the dinner-party—saw it from the wood the other side of the lawn—and decided there and then that he would polish off all six of the people sitting round that luxurious table. It *was* luxurious. Arden has a very fine taste in food and wine, and he has the money to cultivate and indulge it. One look at the table would have convinced our madman that he had come to the right place. So he plumps for the host—the man responsible—the richest-looking of the lot.

Blake.—The thing began before that. The previous night Hamish Page was shot at.

Skinner.—Hamish Page! Who was even richer, who was an even worthier object of his bullets! It was your notion to begin searching for the motive at the dinner-party. Why not go further back? The fact that those six people were eating a meal together was just as likely to be incidental as not. Suppose the madman was originally someone whom Page had injured? According to all accounts, he upset innumerable people while he was engaged in making his fortune. Arden told me that at least four suicides were caused directly by his money-juggling within a year of his coming to the City. Suppose, as I say, the madman bore his grudge against Page in the first place, but, having killed him, discovered the grudge to have grown too big for its boots, as it were. Unsatisfied, it ran amok, and he proceeded to destroy the friends with whom Page was surrounded. Why should that bullet have been necessarily aimed at Arden? Page was not dead yet, and Page was sitting within a few feet of Arden. Everybody has assumed from the very beginning that the attempt was against Arden.

Blake.—Every subsequent bullet was much too accurate, to my mind, to make that likely. Much too accurate. In fact it's that sort of thing, and the careful deliberation, the silence and the extraordinary immunity from detection, which makes me doubt the murderer's madness. He can't be mad.

Skinner.—There you are wrong. Ask any alienist, any specialist in mental disease, and he will tell you that one of the chief characteristics of a certain type of criminal lunatic is a high degree of cunning. Sanity seldom produces its equal in depth and ingenuity.

Blake.—Well, I was hoping, sir, you might have come to a more definite conclusion about this business.

Skinner.—To tell you the truth, I have only just begun to think about it. I've had other things to deal with, and other troubles. I went to see the Ipswich lawyers about Page's Will, for instance. You see, we need all the money we can get hold of, now that the W.O. people are fighting shy. I wanted to find out how Anita stood with regard to the inheritance. That was before I knew she was dead—actually she was dead at the time I was talking to them—and when it looked as though she might be implicated in Page's murder. The police thought so, and I wanted to know, should she be found guilty, whether the money she inherited under his Will could be taken away from her, or her next-of-kin.

Blake (with a rise of tone which blurred the reproduction).—

My God, you are a swine! You thought of a thing like that when you knew they suspected her!

Skinner.—Quietly, Jimmy, quietly! I had already sent for Critchley-Jenkins to deal with that aspect of the matter.

Blake.—That be damned! Where is the man, anyway? He hasn't come, and Anita's dead—murdered! I'm in this two by four hole half underground, and her murderer is free!

Skinner.—Critchley-Jenkins is in Italy. They telephoned me this afternoon.

Blake.—Oh, get out of here! Leave me alone! You've sickened me for years. And if it hadn't been for Anita, I'd have cleared out long ago! You're hard, my God, but how hard! You've devoted your intelligence to the destruction of your fellow-men; you think you're a great man, but you're no better than a great monster! If I hadn't been in the Manor garden half last night, hoping to make sure that nobody shot Anita, I'd have said you'd killed her to get Page's money! But you didn't come. I know that. I watched the house from a tree by the path from Inderswick. She was dead before I got there, of course—was lying murdered while I watched, and the policeman patrolled the garden. God knows how it was done——

Skinner (after a pause).—You've got to get some sleep, Jimmy. You were up all night, and you're heading for a collapse. There's a lot of work for us to do when this stupid business is over, and I don't want an invalid for an assistant.

Blake.—When this stupid business is over you can look for another assistant. If they don't hang me—and they can for all I care—I'm going to Africa.

Skinner.—Don't be a fool! Pull yourself together.

Blake.—Get out! Get out! Get out! I'm going to Africa!

"We took the dictaphone away at that point," said the Inspector. "The Professor knocked at the door to be let out. He was in a state of considerable anger, and stalked out of the police-station without a word to anybody. Blake was all in. I telephoned for Allis, who gave him a sleeping draught. He was not much better this morning, and I've had him taken over to the Cottage Hospital. It looks like a nervous breakdown, or the beginning of one. Allis thinks he can avert it, though. I hope he does. He's a decent youngster, and I'm sorry for him. His world has come a bad smash."

Jupp nodded.

"So he was in the garden last night, was he? He assumes that the girl was killed before he arrived, I suppose, because nothing happened to arouse his suspicions while he was there. I'm afraid it doesn't establish anything, except that the constables did their job conscientiously."

"I can't understand," I said, "how Blake came to decide that I might be the murderer."

"Jealousy, shock, mental disturbance—there are several good reasons," said English. "But I would like to know, Mr. Jupp, if that conversation between them tells you anything?"

"Several new facts emerge," he replied, but he did not, however, enumerate them. He went to the window, and stared out across the sunlit gardens. The Inspector packed up the dictaphone, while I wrote a couple of paragraphs of this account and made a few notes for reference when I came to the dictaphone part. The telephone rang while we were thus engaged, and I picked up the receiver.

It was Professor Skinner.

"Give me Jupp," he said, without inquiring who was answering him.

I hesitated, and then called Jupp from the window.

I left the room and, hurrying downstairs to the telephone instrument in the hall, which is on the same line as the one upstairs, listened with no shame at all to what the Professor had to say to Jupp. There had been a certain terseness in his demand for the detective. I do not know what his first words were, for it took me several seconds to reach the other telephone, but I do not think they were important. I heard:

". . . I shall come straight over now, probably escorted at a respectable distance by the Inspector's minions."

"All right," said Jupp. "I'll wait for you."

There was a click, and then silence. The Professor was undoubtedly one of the central figures at the moment, now that Blake was out of the game, and, although I had no desire to be discovered overhearing a private telephone conversation, I had decided that the risk ought to be taken. When I got back to the study, Jupp was again inspecting the view, and the Inspector was in the middle of reporting the various measures he had taken for the protection of various people, myself included; for the watching of the Professor; for the searching of the countryside by an enlarged and more or less armed body of men; and for the circumvention of the great British Public's desire to lend a hand. The Blythburgh road was now closed to all but legitimate traffic. Jupp did not tell me that the Professor was on his way over, and I announced my intention of shutting myself up in the workshop under the stairs for the next hour or so.

"I've written enough for the time being. I don't want to get stale, and a little fiddling with the insides of that clock you saw me with yesterday will give me a holiday."

"Good idea," said Jupp. "May we use this room for a bit, if you're not wanting it?"

"As long as you like."

"You won't be going out?" the Inspector asked.

"Definitely no. I'm not frightened, but there's a certain devilish unexpectedness about our murderer, and I shall feel happier for a few walls about me."

He commended my wisdom, and I went downstairs, leaving them to their plans and discussions.

Twenty-five minutes later Professor Skinner, walking quickly, his hands folded as usual behind his back, and followed, to quote the phrase he had used over the telephone, "at a respectful distance" by two plain-clothes detectives who had been instructed not to let him out of their range of vision day or night, came along the cross-country path from "Windy Arbour." He passed in safety through the oak wood beyond the garden, and reached the Manor House drive, where he was seen by one of the patrolling constables, who made a point of assuring himself by a close scrutiny that he was not carrying, visibly or concealed under his coat, a ·22 rifle. The constable exchanged a sign of recognition with the plain-clothes men, continued his leisurely tramp round the house, and turned the corner of the south wing.

Except for the two men following the Professor—and they were some way behind him—there was no one in that part of the garden when he came to the point in the drive, thirty odd yards from the front door, where he stopped abruptly, wavered uncertainly on his feet for a brief moment, spun round, and fell face downwards without a cry.

I presume it was the sudden shout of one of the shadowing detectives which alarmed Jupp in the study upstairs, or else he was at the window watching the Professor's approach and saw him drop. At all events I heard the clatter of his feet along the corridor and down the stairs immediately above me as I picked up a brass pendulum rod and began polishing it. Then the small door of the workshop was flung open, and he confronted me. I use the word with intention, for that was what he did. He confronted me with challenge in his eyes. I looked up from my work and stared at him.

"What on earth's the matter?" I asked, and rose from my stool.

For perhaps the first time I was able to read his thoughts. He was demanding of himself—of me:

"How did you do it?"

Then, because he knew the futility of putting the question into words, he turned and hurried into the hall. I kept at his heels.

"For Heaven's sake, Jupp," I asked, "what's happened?"

He had to tell me, gazing along the length of the hall at the closed door.

"Skinner is lying dead in the drive out there."

"Good God!" I said.

"I was down here within twelve seconds," he muttered, and for the second time favoured me with one of his penetrating, challenging glances.

I knew I had succeeded again. He did not know how I had learnt that Skinner was coming to the Manor House; he did not know how I had managed to shoot the man, judging the moment of his arrival to a few minutes and yet be back in the workshop with the rifle hidden again before Jupp himself, morally certain of my guilt, could reach the workshop.

He gazed at the front door because he wondered whether I had opened it in order to fire the shot, and if I had, whether anybody had seen me; he looked at me because he knew I had killed the Professor and that once again my method was going to be difficult to discover.

Then the Inspector came heavily down the stairs, his face a mask of horror.

"He isn't in his room——" he began, and broke off at the sight of me.

"Who isn't?" I asked, but, although neither of them answered me, I knew that the moment Jupp had realised what had happened, and himself rushed downstairs, he had sent English to my bedroom, which overlooked the drive, to see if I was in it, a rifle in my hand.

Jupp opened the front door at last, after a few moments which seemed an age, and we saw the plain-clothes men bending over the Professor's body. We went out to them, English glancing at me sideways, sheepishly, as though wishing to dissociate himself from Jupp's fantastic suspicions. Jupp, apparently, had been explaining his theory, so difficult of proof, to a police inspector who found himself unable to believe that John Arden, Lord of the Manor of Eastblyth, Chairman of Trustees of the East Suffolk Police Orphanage Endowment, and an eminent sociologist, was at all likely to have committed four, nay five, horrible murders.

I realised that if Jupp had known I was aware of Skinner's impending arrival he would have kept his theory for a later moment. He would never have allowed me out of his sight for a second. I had tricked him, and he realised I had tricked him; the fifth and last murder had been committed.

Even the incident of Jeames being somewhere in the attics

at the time the Professor was shot could scarcely be produced as part of my deliberate plan—and yet it had been. It had been a simple matter to send him to look in the lumber-room for the grandfather clock case to which belonged the works I had just finished cleaning. He actually came slowly down the stairs with the thing on his shoulder as Jupp reached the hall again. Jupp scowled at him.

"Here it is, sir," Jeames said to me a little breathlessly.

In the meantime the garden was alive with people searching, people who were more frightened than they cared to show at this fresh murder in their very midst. I was present a few minutes later when Jupp asked his important question of the plain-clothes men.

"From where you were when the Professor fell," he said, "could you see the front door?"

"Yes, sir."

"Clearly?"

"I could see the brass door knocker," replied one of them.

"All right," said Jupp. "Did the front door open?"

They looked at one another.

"No, sir."

"Sure?"

"As certain as I can be," said the second.

"You heard the shot?"

"Yes." But they had not realised until a moment afterwards that the sound they had heard was indeed a shot. It had not been at all loud—more like an air rifle going off than anything else. They could not say where it had been fired except that it was somewhere in front of the Professor, and not behind him.

The body was carried into the small waiting-room off the hall, and Jupp devoted himself to a close examination of the scene. He was manifestly puzzled. There were no windows on either side of the porch; indeed, the nearest window to my workshop which faced the drive was in the waiting-room I have just mentioned. This, however, was of stained glass in a mullioned setting, a cowled monk holding a fishing-rod, and

Jupp disappointedly realised that it was not designed to open. No rifle could have been put through it without removing one of the small panes, but none had been disturbed.

He looked gloomily at it for a few minutes, and when the Inspector returned from a fruitless search of the grounds he accompanied him to conduct an examination of the Professor's body. I did not go with him, but while they were thus engaged I replaced the three rusty screws which until a quarter of an hour previously had held in position behind the flap at the side of the front door the once-upon-a-time detachable letter-box. In the less trusting times of my grandfather, this had been removable, sliding out of grooves, and when the post came, a servant had carried it to someone in authority to be opened with a key. In these days there is no key, and Jeames merely puts his hand through the little door in the back and takes out the letters.

Jupp had spotted this letter-box as soon as he contemplated the front door, and I knew he came to the conclusion that it might have been through this that I had shot the Professor.

He would find, however, when he came to examine it later, that the little door was six inches below the narrow aperture which corresponds with the outside flap. Whether or not he would be able to tell if the screws holding the box to the woodwork had been taken out and replaced, I could not at that moment tell, but I took great care to rub dirt into the nicks, so that the recent marks of the screw-driver were no longer perceptible.

As to the weapon, I had had ready, in a small secret cupboard in the workshop, the ·22 with its Maxim silencer attached. With Jeames out of the way fetching the grandfather clock case, I was able to emerge into the hall carrying the rifle with little risk of being seen by anyone, and to return to the workshop as quickly as I was able before the alarmed shouts of the man who had seen Skinner fall brought Jupp out of the study and down the stairs. There had been several seconds to spare, but I must admit that only an immediate necessity for the Professor's removal could have induced me to run such risks in its accomplishment. The other murders, although subject to unforeseen accident, were not conducted in the same desperation, and were by their deliberation less likely to lead to my being detected, although in actual fact it was in the killing of Anita that Jupp came upon a point which set him suspecting me. But for that unhappy chance I doubt if he would have ever hit upon the truth. I allude to the fact that because I shot her at rather close range the bullet did not lodge in the skull, but penetrated it completely. (I shot her, of course, from inside the room.) She had backed to the window as she half realised the real import of my appearance in her room, and the bullet passed through her head, out of the window, and fell somewhere in the garden. This was perfectly all right—the girl was dead—but it had been my plan from the beginning that it should seem as though she had been shot from outside, and in that case, if the bullet wasn't in her head, it must be somewhere in the room, either embedded in the wall or lying on the floor, according to the amount of its remaining force. Jupp had pointed out this in his first survey of the affair, and between then and the arrival of the Inspector and Dr. Allis, and while Jupp was dressing, I slipped into the workshop and taking a cartridge from the box in the secret cupboard, prised out its bullet. When I followed Jupp and the Inspector into the blue room I dropped it into the pool of tea which Mrs. Jeames had conveniently spilt just inside the door when she let fall the tray. I did not think that Jupp had looked in the débris of crockery, and it was only later, when P.C. Roberts brought the bullet to our conference, and I saw the fleeting expression on Jupp's face, that I realised that he had. He saw immediately that the bullet must have been introduced into the room *after* his first visit to it. In other words, the murderer had discovered his mistake and done what he could to rectify it, thus making it infinitely worse for me, since the whole thing at once narrowed down to a completely small number of possible people, and of this number I was one, although my motive, if I was also guilty of the murders of Page and Lady

Codrington, remained incomprehensible. That was Jupp's feeling, and he began to try to find evidence to link the three murders together. He seized every opportunity to search the house for the ·22, and I believe he went very thoroughly over the workshop. I do not propose to tell him where that cupboard is; it is a clever cupboard, and it took me as a boy three days to find it, and even then I was helped by a hint my father had given me. At all events, the rifle is no longer in it, but somewhere else, where sooner or later Jupp will come upon it.

Before I go back and review the earlier stages of the affair, I must explain that my desperate need to kill Skinner before he reached Jupp that morning was because I knew, the moment I heard his voice on the telephone, that he had remembered a conversation I had had with him eighteen months previously—a conversation in which I had postulated the moral right of an individual to destroy members of the community whose activities in it, although beyond the reach of the law of the country, were nevertheless obviously anti-social and dangerous to the common good. We had argued; and I had supported my contention with some heat, although we had never again returned to the subject. From the moment James Blake had suggested that I might be the murderer, although he could neither say why I was nor whom my accomplice might be, the acute danger arose that Skinner would begin to consider the possibility, and, in seeking a reasonable motive, remember my theory of eighteen months ago. I was grateful indeed for the opportunity Jupp gave me of hearing the dictaphone record, although, as a matter of fact, I think he wanted me to be present in order that he might study my reaction to Blake's suggestion.

Glancing back over the last few pages I have written, I see that I have used a phrase: "only an immediate necessity for the Professor's removal." This may create the impression that I killed him only in order to prevent his talking to Jupp; and this would be a false one. Certainly it hurried me, and made me take unwelcome risks, but I had decided to kill him several weeks before, deeming him a power for harm at a time when the community—indeed, the whole world—was making its first really serious effort toward international disarmament. His feverish production of invention after invention designed solely for the destruction of life and property—of peace— was contrary to the spirit with which the nations were seeking amity. But quite apart from this, he had contributed largely to the horror and misery of the Great War, and for that reason alone was punishable.

Page was another of these, and his activities, directed only to self-aggrandisement through the medium of money, were all the more reprehensible, since they had had their field at home, where the ardent and continual self-sacrifice of patriotism had supplied him with the opportunities for accomplishing his end. I killed him without compunction, and, I hope, put fear in his heart when I sent a bullet whistling over his head the night before the dinner-party—the night before I actually shot him. Getting him to come to the window was comparatively easy. Before he said good-night to me after the dinner he confessed to the anxiety he was obviously feeling. I took full advantage of the opening, and offered to walk over to "The Towers" some time during the night and make sure that there was no one lurking about. If I found nobody I would throw a stone at his window, and he was to reassure me that all was well with him. He accepted gratefully, promising to tell no one, lest inadvertently he warned the malefactor. The accuracy of the ·22 was again demonstrated to me, and I was glad of the frequent target practice, which I had had purely for my own amusement, with another and slightly larger calibre rifle down on the beaches—throwing tins picked up on the shore back into the sea from which they had come, and sinking them with an ever smaller minimum of shots.

The arrival of George Jupp was a complete surprise to me: I had under-estimated Page's anxiety. It meant that he had sent for aid immediately after the attempt on him. I might have suspected, of course, that he had done something of the kind from the fact that he had made no fuss to the local police. When Jupp introduced himself to me, I recognised him both by hearsay from Bowers of the Home Office, and by ordinary intuition, to be an astute-minded man, and I decided to keep as near as possible to him during his investigations. For this reason I made a point of inviting him to stay at the Manor. At the same time I decided to adhere to my programme as closely as possible, realising that if I could shorten the time between the successive murders, the better would be my chance of accomplishing them unhindered. Five murders are quite a number, and I doubt whether I could have managed them all if I had not already arranged in advance most of the details for them. The letter to Lady Codrington, for instance, written in what was as near an imitation of the Vicar's hand on his own notepaper as I could manage, was one of them. It had been ready a week before I slipped it that night into her letter-box at "Four Ways," confident that she would obey its request and come (with all her romanticism avid and alert) to Brooker's Mill the next morning. Half an hour before she arrived I hid myself in the ruin, and from its shelter shot her before she even realised that her philandering friend the Vicar was not there to keep the appointment he had not made. As she dropped dead amidst the gorse, I reflected that the pornographic outpourings of her neurasthenic soul would no longer pollute clean paper, and that those of the growing generation who read her books would look in vain for more, and perhaps live more decently for the lack. It was as good a morning's work as I had ever done, and I did not regret my somewhat anxious but successful return without being seen by anybody, the ·22, divided into its two component parts of stock and barrel, disposed under my clothes. I put it back in its cupboard in the workshop on my way to join Jupp at the breakfast table. He did not know; nobody in the house knew that I had been farther than the garden, if indeed as far.

Before I deal with the events following the discovery of Lady Codrington's body, I must take the rather complex matter of Anita Skinner, beginning with her sudden and unexpected descent upon me the day Jupp came, when she asked me to get back for her the threatening letter she had written Hamish Page. It was on this occasion, also, that she broke to me the astonishing and disagreeable news that she had fallen in love with me—I say "disagreeable," for it could only be that in the light of my utter dislike and disapproval of her. She was loathsome, really loathsome, and her youth, which in so many asks forgiveness for sins, was in her a sheer affront. She used it shamelessly; indeed, it was her chief weapon. She was not pretty, and save to careless and casual lovers quite unattractive. She played the part of the child let loose on the jam-shelf, who must taste every kind before anyone came. It was this youthful, scatter-brained daring which caught James Blake, who, knowing little of human beings and less of women, saw nothing of the hard, calculating machinery of her real self. Sensual, over-sexed and ruthless, she permitted none of the social decencies to stand between her and the gratification of her most wanton desires. To young men like Blake—young men of worth and promise— her passion was destructive; there could never be love in it, and never tenderness; she would maim and destroy rather than build and inspire. Killing her was not an act of brutal murder, but a social necessity.

I had been fully aware of the millionaire's desire to marry her, but I was quite ignorant of the methods he had been employing to bring this about. To learn of the existence of such a letter as Anita had been driven to write him was a considerable surprise to me, but it was also a pleasant one. If the police found it they might well suspect her, and that they should suspect anybody in particular would mean a greater freedom of movement for me while I continued with my plan. I could not be sure, of course, that Page had kept the letter, but I was certain that if he had they would come upon it sooner or later. I promised quite honestly to try to retrieve it for her, but at the same time I had no hope at all that I would be permitted by Inspector English to do so.

When Jupp came in at the end of our interview, with his announcement that Page had made a Will in her favour, my conviction that she would be suspected became certainty, but I saw, with no comfort at all, that since she had been present at the dinner-party they would begin looking for an accomplice who could have fired the shot at me, and probably also at Page. James Blake would fit this rôle, and, as it later proved, he fitted with remarkable neatness. He could have killed Page because the man was pestering Anita. He could have tried to kill me either because he wanted to remove me as the object of the affections he coveted or in order to make an alibi for the girl. He might have killed Lady Codrington because she had somehow discovered the truth about the millionaire's death. (After all, who could say with certainty that her lush sentimentality, so largely the subject of her life, had been the reason and also the instrument of her death?) It was quite conceivable, also, that Blake might have killed Anita, when he realised that she did not love him, but had gone to the man of her choice, intent only upon escaping, by turning King's evidence, the penalty of her association with a murderer. At all events, there was meat enough in the theory to keep Inspector English busy chasing a wild goose. It effectively drew all his attention, and permitted me continued freedom of movement. Jupp did not begin to see daylight in the affair until after Anita was dead, and by that time I had dealt with three of the five. I think, as I have said before, that it was the incident of the missing bullet which really presented Jupp with the first clue; and yet the fact that the Inspector did not find it in the pool of tea in the course of the second search of the blue room might have suggested, feasibly, that Jupp had overlooked it during the first. But Jupp had scrutinised the mess, apparently, when he was looking for the bullet, and had satisfied himself that the bullet was not there. Also, until the girl's death he had been inclined to follow the police suspicion that she might be implicated, that there were, indeed, several good reasons why she might be—three and a half million of them, indeed, apart from any desire to put an end to Page's amorous persecution.

Thus, with Jupp living in the house and with the Inspector

always inclined to avail himself of Jupp's help and my Sunbeam car, I found myself, to my satisfaction, as intimately connected as I could wish with the efforts made to solve the mysteries. In this, however, there were naturally disadvantages, particularly in the fact that I was continuously called upon to act the part either of the astonished onlooker or the handy authority on local life and conditions. I was prepared, for instance, to hear of Lady Codrington's death at any moment during the day of her murder, but when the news came I overdid my horror and surprise to an extent which brought forth comment from Jupp a little later. Again I had difficulty in concealing my alarm when the Inspector began putting Blake and Anita together, and my efforts to suggest that because my own life had been attempted they could have had nothing to do with it (since Anita had been present and Blake had no hatred of me) must have sounded lame in the extreme. I liked Blake very much indeed, and although I knew that ultimately his innocence would be established, I heartily disliked the thought of his arrest and imprisonment; I could not escape my conscience, which pointed out, with complete truth, that the fault was mine. That it had been unforeseen was scarcely an excuse.

It was in order to rescue the young man that I killed the Reverend Lionel Lake several days sooner than I had originally intended, although I did not materially alter my pre-arranged plan. I had had no difficulty in learning the Vicar's habits, and his invariable hour at his desk before lunch had struck me as being the obvious time to choose. A casual reconnoitre had discovered for me the gap in the hedge of Sandy Lane, and its convenience as far as the study window was concerned. The Vicarage garden was about thirty yards wide at that point, and the lane another three—a range which reduced the likelihood of my missing his head to a fractional chance. With the arrest of Blake, the police guards around the Manor and the Vicarage had been withdrawn; I concealed the ·22 under my clothes, and circumspectly set off at twelve-thirty, at which hour the gardeners knock off for lunch. There was nobody about, and I was able to reach Sandy Lane without being seen. Half in the concealment of the hedge, I assembled the rifle in a few seconds, and, using a nickel-plated bullet as usual, removed the Vicar from the wicked world which he had so often condemned but which in his private and personal life he had done nothing at all to improve. His relationship with Lady Codrington had, in my judgment, placed him beyond the possibility of mercy. His harsh intolerance of the "trouble" in which occasionally some village maiden found herself had exasperated me more than once, and when I discovered that for several months he had been enjoying the surreptitious favours of our local *literateuse* under the guise of spiritual friendship, a friendship with which he told me he hoped to wean the lady from her pagan way of life, I could find no words to express my disgust and horror that such a hypocrite should remain a priest of a Christian religion, and set himself up as an arbiter of right and wrong, a critic of the healthy immorality of the young and ignorant.

I concealed the rifle about my person again, and went quickly back, keeping in the shelter of the woods as much as possible, and entered the Manor by the drawing-room, an unfrequented approach to the hall and the workshop, where I proposed to return the ·22 to its hiding-place. It was with considerable surprise and some discomfiture that I found the Professor in the room, waiting for me. Like everybody else, I supposed him to be in London for the day. I had the rifle barrel down one trouser-leg, and though I could walk without much fear of its being detected, I could not sit down without some risk. I had to remain standing, therefore, while he talked about Anita and the question of Blake's guilt or innocence, and knew that at any moment Jupp might return to lunch. My awkwardness of carriage and disinclination to take a chair, while it would probably escape the Professor's notice, might not escape the more observant Jupp's. Luckily, however, he did not come home until past two o'clock, and I was able to slip into the workshop while the Professor was washing his hands for lunch in the cloakroom off the hall.

The next and logical development was the sudden increase in the suspicion already directed against the Professor by Jupp in his effort to produce an alternative theory which would clear Blake. The Inspector, taking into consideration the fact that the Professor had said he was going to London, but had actually only gone as far as Ipswich, returning to pass at the approximate time of the murder within a hundred yards of the Vicarage window, became very ready to agree with Jupp that the man had had both opportunity and motive for at least three of the four murders—also a choice of weapons, since "Windy Arbour" had housed ·22 rifles in bewildering profusion. It could not be ignored, on the other hand, that there was no story, as with Blake, of target practice on the beach, and that it was scarcely likely that Skinner would murder his own daughter, however much she reminded him of a wife who had deserted him a decade previously, and however richly he would benefit by her death. It was just a trifle incredible. But again there was Jupp's idea about "The Silent Skinner." I do not know whether Jupp himself ever seriously believed in it, but the Inspector saw it as the first sensible solution of the attempt to shoot me on the night of the dinner-party. It had the great virtue of doing away with the necessity for an accomplice: the Professor could have played a lone hand from the beginning.

In connection with that attempt, by the way, it is interesting to reflect that Jupp's remark, made quite early in the affair, that it might have been an alibi-maker, was remarkably accurate. It was the most satisfactory method I could find of diverting attention from myself as the murderer; as one of the victims, or near-victims, I would enjoy immunity from suspicion and become a person to protect rather than question. [This indeed happened, and the police patrol in the Manor gardens might well have interfered with my plans; I might have had to wait for days, perhaps weeks before being able to move about at night. For this reason I seized the opportunity presented by Anita's desire to sleep at my house the night she had tried to run away; it obviated all need for awaiting a chance to get to "Windy Arbour" unseen.]

To revert to the attempt to shoot me on the night of the dinner-party, it was not difficult to engineer. My accomplice was no more than an American alarm clock of a well-known make and accurate time-keeping quality, which I screwed on to the butt of the ·22, having first removed the alarm hammer. To the spindle of the wheel designed to actuate the hammer I tied a piece of thread, of which the other end was attached to the rifle trigger. I had filed down the cam of this so that only a slight pressure was required to pull it, and after a few experiments I was able to set the alarm dial of the clock so that I could tell to within a few seconds the moment the tightening thread would fire the rifle. It was a matter of no difficulty to fix the rifle in one of the trees on the edge of the wood, above the height of a man and out of sight from the ground, and aim it at the exact spot on the panelling behind my chair in the dining-room which I wanted the bullet to hit. Incidentally I chose a lead in preference to a nickel-covered bullet, lest it should penetrate the panelling, and be difficult to retrieve; I wanted its calibre to be ascertained, and, later on, its relation to subsequent bullets recognised.

The night of the dinner-party was warm, and the moonlit view of the lawn and trees as beautiful as it could be; it could have occurred to no one to challenge as unusual the open windows and curtains. Having synchronised the grandfather clock in the dining-room with the alarm clock on the rifle-butt, it was necessary for me merely to keep my eye on the time. I was alert for the bullet. I heard the whirr of its arrival, and with my fingers snapped the stem of my wine-glass almost simultaneously with the thud with which it struck the panelling. The breaking glass added to the dramatic element of the incident. I had apparently been within an inch or so of sudden death.

Skinner, as I had rather expected, became at once the expert; he diagnosed the affair with a clarity which did nothing to lessen its seriousness, and by the time Jeames had closed the windows and drawn the curtains, and Sergeant Grice had been sent for, the attempted murder occupied all their minds with anxiety and horror.

Page's account of the bullet which had passed over his head the previous night put the finishing touch to the sinister mystery. He and I were the victims of a conspiracy, and sympathetic eyes were turned upon us. I was safe from the vaguest breath of suspicion.

I still believe that if I had had anyone else but Jupp against me I might have completed my self-allotted task and successfully escaped the consequences. When the idea first occurred to me, when I looked round my Eastblyth neighbours and acquaintances and saw them suddenly for what they really were, I realised that in removing them one by one from further opportunity of evil-doing I would be running considerable risks, but I decided that the object was worth it. I would be devoting my energies to better purpose thus than by writing yet another sociological work for other sociologists to read—it being quite certain that no one else would, for they never do.

For once my sociology would be purely and satisfactorily practical.

At the time, then, I believed that if I was careful and kept my head, I stood a good chance of coming safely through the inevitable inquiry.

But Jupp has realised the truth, and since I do not propose to invite the stares of the horrified and the endless boredom of helping some eminent King's Counsel to fight for my life, which I no longer particularly desire to continue—the strain of the last few days had made me very tired—I intend to make an end of it in a fitting, and perhaps not inartistic manner.

JOHN ARDEN

Note by Detective-Inspector George Jupp, of the C.I.D.

The suicide of Mr. John Arden occurred during dinner last night. A bullet entered the room through the partially opened french windows and the small gap in the curtains covering them, and struck him in the head. He fell back in his heavy chair and was dead before I could get to my feet.

He had taken a stroll in the garden before dinner, and when the policeman on patrol duty was in some other part of the grounds he had fixed the ·22 rifle, with its clockwork attachment on the butt, in the same tree as he had used for his masterly alibi-making effort on the night of the 10th. On this second occasion, however, he trained the sights on the armourial carving on the back of his chair in the dining-room, a chair which was seldom moved on account of its great weight. At seven minutes past nine he leaned his head against the coat-of-arms of the Arden family, and calmly waited for the death which he knew must come within a few seconds.

He was, of course, mad, and suffered from that by no means rare delusion of insanity which causes the subject to believe himself particularly, and sometimes divinely, appointed to dispense summary justice.

I am still in considerable doubt whether I could have amassed sufficient evidence to convict him of the five murders he committed, for, in common with so many madmen, his foresight and cunning were of a remarkably intelligent order. His gift for psychology was considerable, and his accurate understanding of the different types of mind with which he was dealing rendered him a singularly dangerous man.

I have recently learnt that the great fortune left by Hamish Page is to go to the State, as there are no Skinners of the Professor's family to claim it and no Pages to contest the Will. I think this detail would have pleased Arden had he known about it, for however misguided his actions, in principle he had his heart firmly directed toward the public good.